Far From Cibola

Far From Cibola

Paul Horgan

with a note by the author

Introduction by Max Westbrook

A Zia Book

UNIVERSITY OF NEW MEXICO PRESS

Albuquerque

To

PHILIP STEVENSON

INTRODUCTION

The artist needs experience. He needs to know first-hand the people and places he is to write about. At the same time, he must remove himself from that experience and reflect upon it with objectivity. If he writes from secondhand experience, his characters tend to be sterile figures, lifeless illustrations of ideas. If he writes from experience but lacks the objectivity necessary to select and change and control, his stories tend to be literal or partisan and, in either case, ephemeral.

The achievement of the desired combination of the subjective and the objective is something that goes on, largely, in the head of the artist; but Paul Horgan has doubtless found a healthy assist from living in and knowing intimately a variety of experiences in two quite different geographical locations. He was born August 1, 1903, in Buffalo, New York, the son of Edward Daniel and Rose Marie Horgan, both second-generation Americans. He attended a private school, showed an early interest in history (he was especially fascinated by Abraham Lincoln), and retains the Catholic religion of his parents. When he was twelve, his family moved to Albuquerque, New Mexico, in an effort to restore the father's health; and in 1919 young Horgan entered the New Mexico Military Institute in Roswell, where he became good friends with his classmate Peter Hurd, who later became a distinguished artist. About this time, Horgan also studied voice and wrote music, art, dramatic, and literary criticism for his hometown newspaper. Upon the death of the father in 1923, the family returned to Buffalo. From 1923 to 1926, Horgan worked on the production staff of the Eastman Theater in Rochester, New York.

Thus, at quite an early age, Paul Horgan had rather extensive knowledge of and experience with New York, New Mexico, Catholicism, military life, art, music, drama, history, and—of course—literature. Having chosen what might be called artistic experience in lieu of college, he returned to the New Mexico Military Institute in 1926 as librarian, serving his apprenticeship as a writer, before publishing his novel *The Fault of Angels* in 1933 (the sixth to be written, the first to be published). Following World War II, during which he became a lieutenant colonel, in 1959 Horgan was appointed a fellow of the Center for Advanced Studies at Wesleyan University in Connecticut and served as director of the center from 1962 to 1967. He received the Harper Prize Novel Award for *The Fault of Angels* in 1933; Guggenheim fellowships in 1945 and 1949; the Pulitzer Prize in History and the Bancroft Prize of Columbia University for *Great River: The Rio Grande in North American History* in 1955; and, in 1973, the Distinguished Achievement Award of the Western Literature Association.

Facts about the education and achievements of Paul Horgan, of course, are merely outward signs of an artistry that readers must see for themselves. According to William Pilkington (*My Blood's Country: Studies in Southwestern Literature*), Horgan's art is

INTRODUCTION

vii

at its best in the short story "To the Mountains"; the short novel *The Devil in the Desert;* the suite of stories *The Return of the Weed;* the novel *The Common Heart;* and *Great River,* that "justly praised" study of the cultural history of the Rio Grande. Critic James Day, author of the Steck-Vaughn pamphlet on Horgan, is particularly impressed by the short story "The Hacienda," *Main Line West,* and *A Lamp on the Plains.* Among my own favorites are *Things as They Are, Whitewater,* and the novel in hand, *Far From Cibola.*

Consistently respected and often praised very highly, this fine short novel may be called characteristic of Horgan's fiction, provided we make allowances for the enormous range of his interests. Franz Vosz in *Far From Cibola,* for example, could profitably be compared with Billy Breedlove in *Whitewater.* The mob at the courthouse is like the more violent mob in *Main Line West.* Both *Far From Cibola* and *Whitewater* include the primal act of climbing to a dizzying height. The ways in which the contrasting lands of New Mexico affect people, the history and legends of the Southwest, the journey of youth toward adulthood: all are important concerns in *Far From Cibola* and in many of Horgan's other works. The points of comparison could be extended for a considerable length, but the two most important entries would have to say something about the episodic technique of *Far From Cibola* and—appropriating a term from art—"magic realism," a concern for the mysteries of the visible world.

In his use of the episode and in his attention to mystery, Horgan may have written—I feel an urge to say "painted"—more organically than we realize. *Far From Cibola* is built from episodes, true enough. Each of the first six chapters, about forty percent of the novel, introduces a new set of characters; and, with the possible exception of "The Three Sons," each of these opening chapters could stand quite well as a separate and complete short story. Still, I do not think that *Far From Cibola* is an episodic novel. It is, rather, a tightly structured novel which tells a single and unified story, though not by the device of a main character or two. The design of the book is highly formal: separate opening episodes flow inward to a common dramatic center, after which all resume their initial stories and flow outward toward a circumference completing both the individual and collective lives of the book's inhabitants.

Basic to the organic unity of the novel is Horgan's attitude toward mystery. The Seven Golden Cities of Cibola are symbolic of one of man's oldest illusions: the eternal passion for fabulous cities of untold riches, gold to be had from the very streets, if only the courageous adventurer can find them. In *Far From Cibola*, however, no character is searching for Seven Golden Cities, and the gold that is said to be in the courthouse is only a brief rumor. The facts of the novel are the facts of the Great Depression of the 1930s, and what is really desired is flour and bacon from the federal government or a free ticket to supposedly helpful relatives in California. Horgan's theme, his treatment of the passion and lure of sudden treasure, is his own redaction of ancient myth, just as his use of varied sets of characters is his own way of achieving artistic unity.

In the opening chapter, widow Ellen Rood finds her two young children, Donald and Lena, caught by the fearful and hypnotic presence of a rattlesnake. While Donald holds the snake at bay with a stick, Ellen sends Lena for the axe and then manages to kill the snake. Ellen and Donald agree the snake will "not die until sundown," and that, in fact, is exactly what happens. In general, the snake represents evil, a part of life; and its death only at sundown implies that it will be born again tomorrow, though in some altered form. Specifically, the snake represents an evil in each human being, a potential that can break out at any moment. In still another sense, the snake is a specific character in the novel.

To identify this character, we must understand that romantic folklore about snakes, like the romantic folklore of Cibola, is material for Horgan, not his subject. The mysteries of primal experience are for Horgan what William Faulkner called the writer's "lumberyard," recorded experience to work with, tools of the trade. Horgan's real subject is the human experience, the primal and the mysterious operating in the ordinary lives of the actual world. In welding ancient mystery with the actual lives of workaday people, Horgan has written a lyrical and organic novel devoted to a dramatic definition of Cibola and snake, hunger and fear, and a variety of human responses to these.

At the heart of this definition is Horgan's recognition of the power of independence. By contrast, the dependent person is one who cannot face the harshness of the actual world. Admirable characters in the fiction of Horgan—whether soldiers like Matthew Hazard in *A Distant Trumpet,* domestic heroines like Ellen in the present novel, or a humble and remote servant of God like Father Louis in *The Devil in the Desert*—are in and of the world. They appreciate its beauty while being fully aware of its treachery and indifference; and they are, above all, independent, able to function despite fear, to see values beyond the temporal, willing to lose and even—sometimes, like Andrew Lark—to gamble in the way of the mischievous boy, as if to prove they are so independent they do not husband too smotheringly close the precious gift of life itself.

The least admirable is the character who rejects life, in part from fear of losing, basically from a smallness of soul which quails before the awesome mysteries of life (like Cibola, like the snake) which can appear in forms that vary from the mighty to the trivial. And thus it is, bringing his narrative argument full circle, that Horgan describes Leo extrinsically as a coward, just as the southern bully is a coward (as suggested by the plural in the chapter title, "Cowards"), but intrinsically, through imagery, as a snake, that is, as a victim of life and of his own lack of strength.

Leo shivers "at the fleshless articulation of himself," as a snake can jerk in a disturbingly unhuman type of spastic movement. His "strength, physical force and

private will," Horgan writes, are "all gone." His very
appearance, like a snake's, is repugnant to people. His
smile is taken for a sneer. The only thing he has left is
self-pity, a turning in on himself—again, the rejection
of life. His voice is a "weak whimper." His only action
is that of the beggar, the pitiful tyranny of the pauper,
confronting others with the plea of his own helplessness. Like his primal counterpart in the opening
chapter, he has inadequate covering and cannot "die
until sundown."

And Leo's story is not a vignette, an episode. Mrs.
Vosz is another version of the tyrant of weakness,
clinging to her three sons by the appeal of self-pity.
Mrs. Rocker, another, is used by Horgan as a brief and
bland mirror, a grotesque *Doppelgänger* of Fat, who is
still another version of the tyrant of weakness. She
provides Fat an unwanted glimpse of his own self-
pity, an audience for his cheap bullying of the begging Leo, and an occasion for evasive outbursts and
rationalizations of the decision he and so many other
Horgan characters (Mainwaring in *A Distant Trumpet,* for example, or Father Pierre in *The Devil in the
Desert*) are too cowardly to make.

Ellen, in her modest way, is the opposite of Leo,
and her story foretells the structure of the novel. First,
she is described as having a "strange" contentment,
strange because her life is so drab, but contentment
because she belongs *to* her world, finding peace in the
everyday chores of hearth and home. Then comes the
incident of the snake. Next, Ellen's "love of independence" is reaffirmed. Her chapter ends with Horgan's

sudden and brief mention of the Seven Golden Cities of Cibola and the association of the legend with the mysteries of the New Mexico land.

Something comparable—and it would be interesting to trace the similarities and differences in detail—happens to Mr. and Mrs. Lark, Heart DeLancy, the Vosz family, Fat, and—in the scene before the courthouse—to the town, with established characters indicated at first by details and not by name, to stress the general nature of the personal experience. In short, the snake, or anti-life, is always present, always a threat. Cibola, a dream of something filled with wonder, is also a part of life. Like all dreams of wonder, it is filled with questions: Is it dream only, or do people like Andrew Lark and Franz Vosz achieve at least a touch? Is the California illusion of Leo a definition of Cibola or merely what Cibola is to Leo? Is the edge of mob violence a touch of the evil of Cibola, and, if that is so, why do the effects, for some, seem to be salutary? Is the cruel accident in the scene at the courthouse an earned result for those who listen to rumors of easy gold or a tragedy set in motion by response to privation?

Answers, like gold, seldom come easily, but it may be that Cibola, for Horgan, is largely what the individual makes it to be. Historically, the Spanish quest for Cibola was teased onward by numerous reports—supposedly factual and firsthand—that the rumors of gold were fact and not rumors. When the explorers finally reached Cibola, however, all they found was rolling plains and grass, a crushing disappointment for those who lust for gold, but something altogether different for pioneers in search of a home. What is found by the individual characters in *Far From Cibola* may have a great deal to do with the individual's personal version of the universal dream of magic treasures.

Max Westbrook
Department of English
The University of Texas at Austin

AUTHOR'S NOTE

Far From Cibola In Retrospect

In my late youth or early middle age—where is the line?—I daily saw the places and persons of this novel, and I witnessed, though mercifully I was not hurt by it as they were, the central circumstance of their common life, which was the hardship caused by the economic depression of the 1930s. What they endured, how they tried to bend trouble to their wills, and find deliverance, and how their suffering found expression, I was able to feel by being there. Though my novel was written some time after its events, I contained these, it seemed, as though they were seeds which must burst their pods and assume new form in my work.

At the time of which I write, I was in the small city of Roswell, New Mexico. Now fast-growing, prosperous and diversified in its resources, Roswell was then feeling the depression. A county seat, it was also the home of the New Mexico Military Institute—"the Institute," as the townpeople always spoke of it. I was an officer of the school, which was then the city's chief ornament and source of business. For the rest, Roswell was a trade and marketing center for the cotton farmers of the Pecos Valley and the cattle and sheep ranchers on the plains farabout. When the depression settled over the land, the ranchers, farmers and small businessmen felt hardship grow steadily and fast.

I used to see them when they came to town on
Saturdays to stand around on the corners of Second
and Main or to gather on the Courthouse lawn, and I
would make little wash drawings of some of them as I
remembered them later. Their troubled thoughts
wondered visibly in their faces. Presently I found that
I was adding to their persons the characteristics of
other people I knew and when my novel came to be
written, it almost wrote itself, so ready was my design,
so acute was the sense of need in life which anyone
could feel among our citizens in that time, and so
filled were my characters with the pity and urgency
of universal human wants as these encountered qual-
ifying difficulties from without. It is my recollection
that I wrote *Far From Cibola* in twelve consecutive
days of entire possession by its form and its echo of
the passionate effect of human lives upon each other
when all desires have a common object.

On those Saturdays when people gathered on the
Courthouse lawn to take comfort from discussing
their shared troubles, occasionally an orator arose
among them. Inspired by the hunger of the family he
was responsible for, he would lift his voice in the accents of the revivalist, and speak for all. Government
relief was often mentioned, and in fact the New Deal
was moving its machinery of mercy into action. But
help was slow to come, and one day an electrifying
report went through town.

There was a crowd forming, it was said, and the
people were going to march to the Institute on North
Hill. There they would break into the armory where
the cadet regiment's rifles—"government property"—

were locked in racks, seize the rifles, and at gun point demand food for the hungry, of whom, or what agency, none could say. The more prosperous citizens, looking grim, said that revolution was in the air. The military and civil authorities braced themselves for an assault, if it should come; but it never came. An extremity of meaning in the trouble of the times had exploded in rumor—and that was all. But perhaps it was useful. Government relief presently began to be effective.

This threat of violence in the human condition of the time was what suggested to me the beginning of riot in the courthouse scene of *Far From Cibola;* and when my sheriff fired his bullet into the cottonwood treetops to shock his fellow-citizens back to order, my young athlete's accidental death followed as a comment upon the sorrows of disorder and the witless tragedies inherent in power.

In its early seasons this book was appropriated by some critics as an example of the proletarian novel, which was then so drearily fashionable. I declined such classification then, and I formally repudiate it now. This book has nothing to do with masses, or classes, or crippling concepts of man as a being without soul. It is a poem with as many subjects as it has characters; but the subject underlying all others, though never stated, is human charity—"the greatest of these."

Paul Horgan
1962

CONTENTS

The

1.

UNTIL

SUNDOWN

FAR TO THE WEST, THE MOUNTAIN WAS SHINING LIKE glass in colour and mystery upon the horizon. Smoke from morning fires vanished against the sky, pierced by the sunlight. In her kitchen, Ellen Rood laid wood in her stove. The children were in the yard, and their mother could hear the noises of their early work. Donald was hacking at wood with the huge axe that wobbled in his grasp. His sister Lena, with delicate childish movements, washed her hands and face in the tin dish that stood at the edge of the well. Mrs. Rood blew upon her fire, and though the smoke rolled back into her eyes, and sparks burned upward to sting her arms, she hardly noticed them. The children sounded happy, and in her own mind there was a strange content, for when the jobs of her household were going forward, she forgot the various halts in her life which made her experience. At least winter was over, and she would have no more strife with cold for many months. The summer would see Don grow a little more, and the farm let into their cupboards a little more food.

But behind such precarious comforts as these, Ellen Rood considered the promise she had made to Mr. Haystead in town yesterday. Everyone she knew was going to be in town this morning at ten o'clock. She had tried to avoid giving her promise to Haystead. Some pride held her back, perhaps it was Haystead's smiling fury, an expression like a threat, that had offended her love of independence. When he spoke of the Government relief, his small blue eyes went dry, and a little red. His big hands trembled on the wheel of his car. She knew that his family had suffered, and that he loved his children.

It made her scornful to see a man shaken so by the common disasters of everyone she knew. But she had agreed to meet before the Courthouse at ten o'clock. There would be several trucks loaded with food, and a government agent to discuss the sale of crops with the men. Ellen's fire now roared up the adobe chimney.

The children were silent.

She called them, not looking for them through the window. She broke an egg into the coffee-pot. Grease exploded in little bubbles of heat in the bacon pan. Ellen said to herself that she was right to make up her own mind. She might go to the meeting, but she would do as she pleased after she got there.

The children hadn't come in. She went to the door. Her eyes were cooled by the light wind. Her breath grew longer in that burdened air of the morning. She called again. She stepped into the sunlight and walked past the house, walls of old adobe with a roof of hammered tin which her husband had made from waste cans a year before he died. A small shed faced her, with glass panes for its front. Here the chickens lived. Walking faster now, she heard a small commotion, a thrashing

behind the shed, and Lena's voice chirping with a
dry excitement. In a moment she saw Don standing on his bare toes, thrusting a pole at a snake that
tried to coil in the shadow of the chicken house.
Lena's hands were laid over her mouth. Both children were pale. The snake, a colour of the ground
in shadow, flowed about the pole and retreated,
thrusting away the loose dirt surface with a terrible constant strength. Ellen swallowed her
breath. A sickness was in her tongue, and she
stumbled forward running, her legs unsteady but
her eye and her mind strong. She kept her voice
quiet so the children wouldn't turn around. She
took Lena by her bony little shoulders that shuddered from sympathy at her mother's touch.

"Get the axe, Lena," said Ellen. The little girl
crying with a heart full of commotion turned and
ran. Don's throat dried and contracted. Ellen
heard him choke. She slid her arms over his brown
thin arms until she could grasp the pole. Her fingers closed on Don's. She could feel his hard body
beat against her own in their joint fight. It gave
her a passionate anger. Stumbling together, inspired by her rage, they stepped into the sunlight,
forcing the rattlesnake back. In the new light, the

snake flashed and dripped with beads of light as if he were wet. The short grasses and the mild dust quivered upward under his lacing retreat. Donald's head was as high as Ellen's chin. His eyes were as sorrowful as her own. Her high cheekbones seemed to have a smile below them always, but her son's mouth, small and delicate, was stern. It resisted threats every day, from hunger and poverty, from natural pride put down by family grief; from private boyish terrors that he might die, and so leave his mother and sister without defense against the trials of living. On Ellen's face there was sweat. Her tongue dried against her teeth. The snake wrapped its golden dusky length against the pole. Lifting her arms, and Donald's, Ellen flung the snake twenty feet away, a streak that became part of the ground when it hit. Behind her Lena's hand pushed against her quivering flesh. Ellen reached back and took the axe.

"Don, stay back with sister," she said, and drew her fallen hair from her eyes and from the white corners of her mouth. She hefted the axe without feeling its weight, and started forward across the brief grasses, walking with a long pace, lunging jerkily like an old woman. In a little hollow of

gypsum stone, white with pure sunlight, the snake
rested ready, his arrow's head fixed. His rattles
sang in the stillness, like a grasshopper in the
weeds by the porch. Behind her Lena cried shrilly
in her throat. The arrow's head moved slightly,
side to side. The bright singing of the rattles loud-
ened and stopped. The snake flew. It dustily struck
the earth. In the confused shadow of her swinging
skirt, where she stepped quickly, Ellen saw the
dust-coloured body turn again into the coil. Panting out loud, sweating like a woman in labour, she
grasped the axe handle with both hands as if it
were the handle of a churn, and brought the rusty
axe head heavy straight down. It was a thump that
wounded the earth, a deep sound. The snake's rattles fluttered. The white belly turned up, and
Ellen moved back again. She turned the axe in her
hand and clove deep with it, cutting the snake behind its crushed head. A faint stench touched her
nose, and entered her mouth, something that
smelled damp and yet dusty, like mold, like a foul
cistern, yet remote, as if it could be the imagined
smell of an illness in herself.

She kicked loose dirt on the snake. The small
rain of dust fell back where the body, bled of its

smooth power, palpitated slowly to calm. Then she turned, dragging the axe behind her, and walked back to the children. Donald came forward on tiptoe.

"Is he dead?" he whispered.

Ellen took his hard thin shoulders and clutched them with her wet hands. She pressed her mouth shut. Tears rolled down to her lips. She shook the boy with a wild trembling strength. Lena was coming forward too. She began to cry again when she looked up and saw her mother's face, so worn, so familiar, assume the shape of a desperate smile now, while tears ran down its pale brown cheeks. The children understood that their mother was angry with them, and relieved, and fuller of love than she had ever been. The three members of the small, hungry family, three people abandoned by everything but their own ties, suffered a moment that lived as an influence forever after in their lives. The boy forgot it in time. But the weeping love of his mother, as a climax to courage, stayed like a picture with him always. The little girl knew self-pity and generosity, a throwing away of feeling to anyone who would take it.

"Come," said Ellen, turning the children to-

ward the house. She took them to their breakfast.
Entering the kitchen, she lifted the old yellow
newspaper on top of the scarred sewing machine
where she worked at times, and saw that her purse
was lying there safe. The children laughed through
the sucking breath of the lowering excitement.
The purse was a black leather bag rubbed to a
worn rust colour on the corners. It was a family
joke, for Ellen referred to it as the "Black Maria,"
a phrase she had heard somewhere. Love of independence, and the agency of independence, these
were shown the children forever by the frightened
concern their mother had for her purse. It had
rarely been a full purse. Now it was empty. Yet it
accompanied her when she went to the village, and
it rang in the mind like a nightmare when it was
missing, with incident fears, pallid courage, and
childish desire to make achievements to supplant
the Black Maria.

The breakfast dishes cooked and murmured on
the stove. Ellen agreed with Donald that the snake
would not die until sundown; when he thought
of that strange fact, his eyes troubled her. Lena
shuddered, hating the snake and all mention of it.
Her brother let thoughts drift in his mind like

dust through fingers, a childhood feeling, which in words might give pictures of the damp hole where the snake lived underground; the gold tracks of its body through sharp grass in the dawn; the eye like a polished grain of sand caught in a drop of milk; the shift of those scales over one another as the body waved flat through the dust; the convulsion of the snake's body all day, the hot day, when the higher the sun rose the more lucent all shadows became, and smells from the desert were forced into the air, while insects made sounds like the air itself, and the snake turned hot and dead to the touch; until sundown, when the smallest grass could feel the cooler wind, and long rays of light bent upward on the horizon, and the dead snake would be at rest, no more treacherous and tried by life.

It was a land where men had to conquer trial and treachery always, the area of New Mexico that shared the plains country and the mountain country, and men deciding to live there chose the small valleys of reluctant rivers, and planted their trees, making a shade over their houses that was the only kind thing for miles around. It was the land of the Seven Golden Cities of Cibola, that had wooed the northward Spaniards so long ago. The natural mystery of plains giving back to the sky a second sunlight and of mountains drawing the horizon up to blue pinnacles dazzled men through three hundred years, and led them up the dry beds of creeks and over the heat lakes toward the Cities of Cibola, whose yellow gates they never found. Crossing the very plains and mountains where the terrible wealth was promised to be, they were always far from Cibola; their hope had no strength in it but greed; and legend was only a powerful mockery. What wealth they ever found in that land was created by man with the earth, and toiled for in obedience to the seasons; just as the human graces of shade trees and windmills had to be brought and planted before the land gave any comfort.

In this year, 1933, the marks of comfort were visible, once the town was in sight. The sky was blue in the slow-running irrigation ditches that dragged cool sandy mud from field to field. It was a cloudless April and the Winter birds were joined by the mocking birds of Spring, that sang all night long on fences and telegraph wires. In the early morning the air was scented with a sweet burdened wind.

2.

SKYWARD

LIVING NEARER TO TOWN THAN MRS. ROOD, THE Larks still belonged to the country. Mr. Lark possessed a windmill that turned above his house and his turkey-run, shrilling and gong-like, a machine that drew upon the sky to bring water out of the ground. On windy nights, the fury of the turned fan and the complaint of the rudder chains woke Mrs. Lark and visited her for hours like pain. Her husband slept, immense and gaunt, while she held her hands on her breast, hoping to quiet the opinions of anger and disloyalty that arose there and made her heart thump. At such times she hated Lark; yet she could not hate him, for the length of their life together, and the vagaries of humour that kept him laughing or smiling into his old age. He dwelt upon memories, and that made her tender toward him; as a woman of labour and family long scattered, she knew the business of pushing the hours of the present to their fullest use. It was boyish of her seventy-year-old husband to be recalling, always, the circumstances of his boyhood, and the scandals of his early youth, the money he had brought West and lost, the feats of stamina he had performed on the range in winter through snow, or up the beds of dry rivers in the wry droughts of pitiless summers.

Yet Andrew Lark sometimes amazed her by conceiving a plan and executing it at once. In the light winds of the morning, in which his great metal flower turned and whined complacently, the idea struck him that if he greased the windmill, perhaps the next windy night would pass without the clatter that Nona Lark always complained of. He told her he was going up the ladder with a bucket of grease, and asked for his glasses.

"Now Andrew," she said, feeling short and helpless, wafting her glance across the pale blue sky
over them, "you know you're too old to climb
them rungs, that's thirty feet to the platform. You
wait till Moses comes out next time. You just wait,
now."

. She saw him walk, the knobs of his joints pulling
the tendons and releasing them jerkily. She knew
from his hunched shoulder that he was smiling
at her. His stubbornness was always irresponsible,
a matter of laughter and sly slaps on her old thick
buttocks if he chanced to pass her. She saw him go
into one of the sheds that he kept so neat out in
back. He emerged soon into the sunlight, wearing
a wide straw hat and a rope slung across his blue
shirt, that was thrust forward by the long bones of
his great skeleton. To the rope was fastened a
yellow pail full of grease and a stick.

"Andrew," she cried, hobbling forward; her face
turned to a bright gold in the sunlight, deepened
by parallel wrinkles, and toned by her freckles.
"Now you stay away from them rungs."

Her cats gathered at her ankles with soft rub-
bings. Lark chuckled breathily and swinging his
long arms that were heavy with bone instead of
flesh, he passed her grinning. When she called

him an old fool, he skipped, grotesquely, almost obscenely, with love of his own contrariness. At the foot of the grey weathered wooden windmill tower, he measured the height with a squint, and adjusted his bucket. He cleared his throat, and she thought angrily that he was about to begin one of his unbearably long monologues, drawing on all his past experience of windmills and their peculiarities. But he stood silent, putting his hands (they trembled, she feared) on the rung at his breast height. Then he started up.

His ascent against the blue broken pattern of sky that showed through the tower scaffold was an unbelievable movement to Nona Lark, standing below. His old legs that passed across the earth with rheumatic trouble, his arms that creaked in supporting a newspaper, were conducting him higher and higher. An absurd flow of pride touched Nona in the throat, and increased her fear. The silver wheel of the mill spun slowly above him, and he climbed to it without pause. Soon his arms were clawing through the square hatch cut in the platform below the wheel. He raised his head above it, and smelled the wind. The wheel, throwing incessant spokelike shadows over this higher world, whistled sedately by his very ear. Looking down, he saw Nona, and waved, as if he had gone on a far journey. A grey sickness crossed his eyes, at the changed colours of his wife, his farmyard, his roof, the bushes and tulips below there. The blood flew away from his sight and his mind. But only briefly. He recovered in time to see Nona wave back, and flop his hand at her whine of worry.

He drew forth his glasses, large black-rimmed circles, and set them on his nose. Then he crawled to the works of the wheel and the center rods, the chains, and the rudder that hummed as the wind shook its silver fin flatness. With his stick, he paddled purple and gold and black gobs of grease upon the bearings of the mill. Turning with the wind, a movement that took a skill of which he was proud, he saw the fan shaft eat the grease and pack it back into the unseen housing where it turned and went soft. He thickened the chains with plentiful greasing where the iron links chafed and squeaked. The wind was melodious in his ears. His zinc windmill with such sharp blades, twisted sailwise to own the wind, filled his heart with pride. Not for years had he been so close to it, for

his boy Moses usually came up to fix anything that
needed it. The mottled pale blue and silver blades
charged and clanged softly as the wheel turned.
That was a sweet noise, not one to keep anyone
awake, a poor farmer's wife, whose old head was
the scene of so many worries, real and invented.
Andrew Lark deliberately avoided looking down
at Nona, for that might suggest to her that he
cared as much as a trotting mare's fart what he
thought of her fears. He made a rich and hearty
job of the greasing. When he was done, and the fan
turned, the chains quivered, without any metallic
sound but only the sound of how the wind was
taken and thrust by, he sat down and pulled out
his newspaper from his trousers pocket. He leaned
against a corner timber of the tower, and began
to read. His incessant habit, it infuriated Nona
now, for the unconcern it displayed. She threw her
apron up to her face and flashed it down again.
She turned back to the house, panting with anger
at his absurdity. Once there, it struck her that he
was up there to grease the thing as a favour to her,
one she had begged to have done by Moses. In her
parlor, troubled by the complexities of which her
life was made, love mixed with exasperation, and
gratitude with terror, she sat down on the ruby-

coloured sofa of plush, and folded her hands against her lips, and sighed until she felt tears rise.

Through the cool dark doorway of the parlor, she could see beyond across the kitchen to the back door, screened. On the screen, haloed with sunlight, the three kittens leaned their forepaws high up, turning their heads sidewise and scratching dimly. The little one, mewing, pressed its pansy face on the screen. Nona left her sofa and went to the cats, thinking the little one was cute's a crabapple. She saw Lark walking toward the shed out in back. Her rising and falling from annoyance and tenderness and fright left her. She was suffused by an inner blush, some reference to their joint past, adventurous and successful. She knew how he felt about going up the mill. It was wonderful.

After breakfast he confessed that he had left his glasses up there on the platform. Her fury was so full at this that she couldn't speak. Her face flooded dark. He laughed. He flung his great flat hand against her breast in playful coarseness. He said he'd get Moses to come back from town with him in the afternoon. Moses would get them down for him. He wouldn't need them meantime. The silver zinnia hummed and flew slowly constant above the warming yard.

Accomplishments; feats of man over nature, control (tension) of universe

3.

TO

UNDERSTAND

ON THE FARTHER EDGE OF TOWN, AT THE FORK OF
the two roads that fed it, one leading to the railroad junction ten miles away and the other to the
transcontinental highway that cut through the
mountain, the long low shed of the cotton compress was a grape red in the early sunlight. The
shed was so low that from a little distance it seemed
to be part of the ground. In the good times, the
trucks backed up to the delivery deck charging
and ripping the air with exhausts, and the white

and brown bales of cotton were rolled down the
incline in a rich procession, while in the low tower
above the shed the steam exhaust pipe blew like
a gun, and the furious presses in the cool shadows
of the building flung downward on the grey cotton
with a wild grunt. Mexicans ran the machine,
laboring half naked, deafened by the explosion of
the exhaust and the echo like a low thunder in
the eardrums, like a shocked blood, when the pressure was released and the baled cotton gorged
forth to the waiting truck.

At the north end of the shed was an office, behind heavy doors. Here the clang and thunder and
scream of the compress machine were slightly
muffled. Yet when the plant was shut down, the
silence was more difficult to stand than the boom
of industry. No one stayed in the long red sheds
but a Mexican caretaker, and the manager, and
Heart DeLancy, his stenographer. But the manager was away, trying to save his business for his
owners. The Mexican was surly from being under-
fed and indulgent of his humours which Heart
thought obscene. She was sympathetic of his penni-
lessness, but the vigilance of her inner eye upon
its own woes took all her emotions.

She was twenty-six years old. Her parents who

had come here from Texas were dead, after raising
her to her teens with intense propriety, naming
her Heart out of sentiment for the love they'd had
as bride and groom, and showing a long picture
over the arc of years of how stubbornness must
fail and turn weak when a man's hopes are time
after time baffled by dry earth, disease upon cattle,
the escape of the railroad through another town
than this, and finally, most astonishing, old age
and fatigue. Heart had worked for herself since
she was seventeen. The results showed plain in her
small brown eyes, which held a wry light, like some
drift of fluid over unchangeable opinion. Her face
was white, the skin drawn over the bones with a
gentle firmness. Her teeth showed always under
her upper lip, protuberant slightly. When she
laughed, it was a cold sound, yet her eyes danced,
and a little flush took her cheeks. Her breastbone
was prominent, her shoulders shallow. She was
slow in her movements, even in her thoughts, but
quick in her feelings, and full of desires, many of
which she had happily fulfilled by her own enter-
prise.

The first of these was to be educated. Her Texan
parents had both been full of intense but incom-

municable opinions about life, the foundation of their experience, the trial at explaining their failure. Heart was convinced that education was the way to conquest of understanding. She had the usual schooling in county schools, and at seventeen, an orphan, had gone to take special work in a business college at Santa Fe. Here she worked as a waitress, supporting herself. Facts poured into her mind and were superimposed upon each other, warming her by their strange presence, and forgotten very soon. But the life she was leading brought her to the conception of another desire, one that she nursed until an inner gaiety arose whenever she considered it.

Seeing the tourists go through Santa Fe, in great cars, with clothes and accents from dim splendid places, she resolved to travel as much as she could her whole life long. She eavesdropped while her diners ate, listening to their tales, gossip, the fall of their speech, not intending to imitate, but desirous only of furthering the boundaries of her life, so bleak in its outline, yet so full of some inherited curiosity and fire at its core.

When she could typewrite and spell, when a little experience had shown her how to behave in an office, she returned to her home, and went to work for the cotton company. Her salary was good. The compress whistled clouds of released steam into the sunlight all day long, for months, years. The warehouse shed space was at a premium. The trucks rumbled off to the railroad ten miles away, bearing cargoes. Sometimes she rode to the junction, named Ramona, and watched the trains, saving her money in her bank account, and her feelings in her mind. At last she had enough money to board the train. She went alone to El Paso, and bought clothes. She went to California. The suffering light in her eyes was lost in her pleasure. She met people easily, talking with men as simply as with women. She spent her entire savings account in a month of investigation of the world. She came back poor, but content, and amazed by her own conversation, which drew authority from the facts she had observed, and sociability from the relaxation of her self-pity.

It was so in the good times.

Now the silence in the office at the north end of the raspberry red shed was a burden against her head. Heart was alone there. The cotton plants in the wide fields were withered and russet, from being unpicked. There was no one to buy cotton. There was nothing to bale. The engines and the steam were cold and silent. Her boss had cut her salary three times. Then he had stopped it altogether, for there were no letters to be written. Yet he had laughingly assured her that she was still the official secretary and left her her key to the office. Here she came daily, to sit before the typewriter, and compose letters to her friends whom she had met on her trip to California. She looked out of the window and could see ten miles Eastward the brushed faint darkness above the horizon that lingered after the train went through Ramona. Between here and there was a tawny space of flat land, green only where artesian wells had been released, or irrigation ditches dug and willows planted. Out of the other window was the mountain, and the highway leading to it, people bounding on fat tires from coast to coast, able to assuage the restlessness that was American in so many of them as a picture, and so individual in Heart.

She had been spoiled for the meagre design of her destiny, which was to live and die on the Southwestern plains, contributing what she could to the life of those small towns. Turned idle, her fingers

unrented for the skill they had learned, she returned to her inner life, yet this time with no
possibility of letting it purge itself in action and
independence.

In town, opposite the Courthouse, was the newspaper office, with large plate glass windows reaching almost to the packed dirt sidewalk. Beyond the
window was a linotype machine, which was oper-
ated by Rolf Kunkel. When she was successful,
Heart had him call for her at the warehouse in the
evening, and drive her home in his car. Other
times, Rolf's shyness took on the quality of valour,
a defiance, covered with blushes and contradicted
by some watering of his pale blue eyes. He was
nearly thirty, she thought. He was tall, and heavy
at the shoulders and waist. His black hair grew in a
formal series of waves to a peak over his left eye.
She liked his large nose, and the biscuit of his chin,
with the long cleft in it. She considered him handsome, and could imagine him in the clothes of a
Californian. She was too crafty to investigate his
mind, preferring the proofs of his value that she
could detect in his body.

Day after day, idle in the office, she dreamed
about Rolf. She passed a succession of plots through

her mind each of which ended with his capture. At first she had thought in terms of marriage. Now, intense and lonely, without aim, her spirit straitened by poverty, she thought in dreamy terms of "illicit love." Rolf Kunkel went with no one else, she knew.

It was a morning like all the others, until the Mexican caretaker came up to the office door. She knew him by his walk, a step-drag, step-drag sound that betrayed his lame foot. She hated him, for he interrupted her empty bliss, and when he walked in she smelled the reek of his age and indifference, and was angry because he was smiling. She asked him what he wanted.

"Pues nada," he said, "nothing," and cuddled his old brown hands against his dirty vest, fluttering them against his belly as if they were captive birds. His smiling went on, and in his throat he made little moans of announcement and awareness. In a moment, Heart heard a car, and leaned to the window. Her pale cheeks reddened, which made the Mexican caper against the wall. Rolf Kunkel was out there. She watched him climb out of the car and come ambling heavily down the warehouse deck. His large face was sober, and she

impatiently wondered what made him look so
stupid. But when he saw her at the window, he
grinned, and his blue eyes filled with shy cor-
diality, a mistiness, and she turned warmly away
from irritation, to meet him, ignoring the Mexican's lecherous imaginings at this meeting.

4.

THE THREE SONS

IF MRS. VOSZ WENT AROUND SAYING THAT SHE HAD nothing left but her boys, then her husband, who was taciturn and opinionated at the same time, thought the same thing, but said nothing. The boys were triplets, seventeen years old, tall fellows, with yellow hair, and blue eyes that darkened with embarrassment or eagerness when they were filled with ambition or excitement. Their names were Richard, Joseph and Franz. It was a matter of

delight to their mother when they left high
school to help on the ranch, of their own free
will. She took their hands in hers and wept upon
their twisting knuckles, staring at them out of
her weeping eyes with a claim upon them that
was almost unbearable, for its intensity, the references it made to the amplitude of her dona-
tion to their living, and the dues which they must
feed back to her in love. But Mr. Vosz, speaking
calmly behind his curtain-like mustache, returned
the boys to high school, and answered the fanci-
ful fears of their mother with a rough tenderness
in his touch upon her.

The high school was one of the few eminent
marks made by man on the tawny land where
the town stood. As the county seat, the town drew
business traffic to the Courthouse, and boys and
girls from surrounding ranches and villages to
the high school. The Vosz triplets were popular
in school, where their physical excellence, the
thrice-repeated image of men growing out of
clumsy sweating boys, whose hands were desirous
and timid, whose minds dwelt upon the ripening
of information with a secret and frantic intention, impressed the other students though they

could not have said how. It was easy enough to admit that the triplets were magnificent athletes, which was true. The teachers sighed over them as much as the girls, for they were famous in their devotion to their mother. It was felt that anyone who was so good to his mother as any of the Vosz boys and was so clever in school, and so furious on the track field, must become a great man.

In the early mornings, Richard and Joseph would get up while a stratum of cool air still clung over the ground, and run a mile, pacing each other, their big chests lifted against the wind of their running, their legs rising and falling like harmonious parts of music. Franz, the other trip-let, liked to sleep late. But his brothers got him up and dragged him out with them, making him practice with them for the track meet, which he disdained, knowing that he could do things with much greater ease than his brothers, and that he needed less practice, but only the desire like an inspiration to do anything, to do it brilliantly. Because he was so simply superior in the ease he had over his brothers, Mrs. Vosz often scolded the other two for picking on him. Their bland faces would laugh out at her, as if this were a

malicious joke, not to be taken seriously. Franz
would thrust his legs impatiently out before him
as he sat down, and Mrs. Vosz, seeing how fool-
ishly she had accused them, would begin to cry,
begging that they not desert her in her poor fat
old age, with her weak heart and her simple needs.
This sentimental attack was even more difficult
than her nagging. The triplets would crowd
around her, stroking her bulging shoulders and
back, making impatient sounds of consolation,
while she let her head with its topknot of pale
thin hair fall against the breast of one of them.
If Mr. Vosz found such a stormy woe in progress,
he whirled the boys away with his immense hand,
and lifted his wife's chin on his wide thumb, looking into her eyes with a sad rebuke for her weakness. She would then control her heart that feared
so many unnamable things, and let her love call
out for acceptance by baking vast cakes and pies,
pampering the boys and their father to excuse
their memories of her tyrannical weakness.

But such moments had their weight afterward,
when the triplets, abroad with boys and girls in
exploration of fun and desire, would lose the
sweet feelings of guilt they owned and find them-

selves hateful for the grief their mother would feel if she knew.

Such things as these didn't show in the pattern of the daily life which people saw of the Voszes. Mrs. Vosz went to her mid-week church parties in town, lamed by the weight her ankles carried, dressed in blue silk that billowed behind as she walked, nodding her head with its party hat that sat high on her faded hair. Mr. Vosz ran the ranch, though no one could sell cows at the price no one was paying. The sheep kept them alive, going at prices which a few years before would have been a rancher's joke. The boys went to school, working afternoons to get ready for the track meet. Richard was a hurdler. Joe ran the short dashes, and Franz ran the mile and did the high jump. The meet was to be held at the high school athletic field, on the edge of town, a sandy flat with a cinder track. Six schools in the region were entering teams.

But Franz still was too lazy to practice mornings. He could hear his brothers get up, and then the scratch of their spiked shoes in the ground outside his window as they practiced starts. He lay awake, with his eyes closed, then he slept

suddenly again, until Dick and Joe dragged him
out for breakfast. The sunlight was drifting slant-
wise across the stove where Mrs. Vosz was busy.
The steam from the coffee pot turned a trans-
parent gold in the light. The light bounded back
from every clean corner of the room. The smell
of breakfast, the virtuous smiles on the faces of
his brothers, the unthought-of familiar shape of
his mother, made Franz very happy, and he leaned
far out upon the table in the kitchen, and thought
of the track meet that afternoon; his stomach contracted pleasantly. It was a sensation that reminded
him of the challenge to his stride, the fact that
he would win, easily, and the simple chance that
he might lose; the love for a physical game that
kept him and his brothers so busy.

Mrs. Vosz brought the cereal bowls to the table.
She set them down and watched the boys pour
sugar and cream on. Their big hands, the hungry
opening of their mouths, waved across her in a
pitiful memory of their babyhood, and she pas-
sionately knew they were the same now as then,
and that their hearts were untouched by the idea
of love, and its consequences, which had drawn
her own life down from girlhood to marriage,

brief rapture and then devoted drudgery, with her mind losing everything but concern for her family, her body heavying, her fortunes lowering with those of her husband. It was some helpless devotion to life and acknowledgment of it that led her into the punishments she made on herself and the boys when she claimed them, over and over, to her own fidelity. After bearing a large family, now scattered into so many separate lives that touched her only incidentally, though she had given them birth, she had borne the triplets, a last terrible ordeal of her body, and a growing nourishment for her heart.

The boys finished their oatmeal. Their spoons scraped and they licked their mouths, looking to her with trust for the next food she had ready. Their eyes were laughing. She brought them their eggs and bacon and coffee, and then she said,

"I know you're good boys, I know it in my heart. A mother always knows."

She knew how they hated any tearfulness, or any of this business about love. Her words therefore sounded angry, for the control she threw into them. Franz slapped the table, and made a joke. They avoided the moment. They remembered

times when they had not been good boys. It made
them angry now to have such times brought up
by what their mother had said. A certain mourn-
fulness, an atmosphere of resentment, drifted over
them in the kitchen. It was broken into open irritation when Mrs. Vosz said,

"How many of my boys are going to town with
Papa and me?"

Joe laid down his fork, and said,

"Mumma, you know the meet's this afternoon."

The other two went on eating. But Franz looked
up and saw the facile hurt expression on his mother's face.

"Mumma, you've known about it for weeks," he
said. "We all three are in it. I'm running the
mile."

"So you see, we can't," said Richard.

"What's happening in town anyway?" said Joe.

"Your father has to go to the Courthouse," said
Mrs. Vosz. "Your track meet's not till the afternoon. We was going in the morning, and to lunch
at the cafe, but I suppose it's too much to ask
for a boy to be seen with his pa and ma."

There was a silence. The morning was recognized as hot, yet with stray tendrils of spring wind

in it. The boys hated this sort of rebuke. Their silence, which was one of good judgment, seemed surly to their mother. She laid her plump hands with the smooth shiny filled skin on her bosom under her great rounded throat, and plucked in anxiety, irritation, at the loose flesh there.

"It's perfectly all right to get up before sunrise and get your breakfasts. I suppose I don't need any praise for that. Nor am I wanting praise." The strange churchy sound of the word praise took her emotions; it reminded her of God, God is love, and sorrowfully she began to weep. The boys knew it from her voice, for they were not looking at her. Their necks reddened. The intolerable justice of their debt, a debt of life and emotion, made them feel a little wild in their minds. But they went on eating, and their mother went on talking. "Oh no, you'd rather go off somewhere by yourselves or with them kids from school, God knows what you do with them, I pray so hard that you keep good and all, how do I know?" she cried, seeing the inevitable betrayal of her jealousies in the images of the triplets, who carried youth's burdens and needed to be rid of them, a need that contained fear and sweetness, a spend-

ing of youngness. "Every chance you get, you run
away from us, you leave your home, God knows
'tain't much: your Papa has done the best he could:
and so've I, not that you care, with your track
meets and all: what is this crazy track meet: you
ought to be on the ranch helping your Papa instead of running to school with them girls. . . ."

Richard pushed his plate away and arose. He
went to his mother and touched her shoulder.

"Now, Mumma," he said.

She sobbed and refused his touch.

The other boys, with a heaviness in their hearts
for the humiliation of their spirits, and yet knowing a necessity of assuaging bitterness, went to
join Richard. They gathered around Mrs. Vosz
and playfully talked to her; they made jokes, and
agreed that they were poor dumb hicks, and didn't
deserve all she gave them. She admitted that her
heart was sore from things that she couldn't de-
fine, and that her temper ran away with her. She
kissed them all, and said she was sorry for thinking mean things about them: she knew they were
good boys, in her heart, she said. They blushed.
Franz, in confusion, said that he would go to
town with his father and mother, and after lunch,

he would go to the track meet. The other boys, he said, were going to spend the morning at the field, practicing. He wouldn't need the practice.

"I'll go with Poppa and Mumma," he said to Richard and Joe. "You hicks better get to work. I don't need the practice."

They all laughed together, and a new geniality came up. Mrs. Vosz kissed Richard and Joe, forgiving them for not staying with her. It was Franz, who did everything so easily, the handsomest, the sweetest, she knew, it was he whom her secret heart loved as the son of whom the three boys were the triple likeness.

5.

INTENTIONS

FAT'S CAFE WAS ACROSS FROM THE COURTHOUSE, and a couple of doors down from the newspaper office. It was the place where occasional transcontinental motorists stopped for lunches and suppers, and where all five of the high school teachers went now and then for a festive meal. In the good times, when the movies were showing twice a week in the Imperial Theatre down the street, Fat had crowds for supper. When the cotton compress was

running, the truckdrivers and the foremen, the
visiting ranchers and farmers all came to eat with
Fat. He composed affectionate little ads for the
paper, "Fat's Cafe, The Lunch Grand," and "Elegance and Home-Cooking, Fat's Cafe," which
brought his appearance and his voice before the
reader's eye. Fat was the owner of a sad face with
a fastidious expression. His flesh flowed in a widen-
ing line from his ears, the button of his chin, his
buried jaws, down upon his breast and back. His
arms were pink and delicately modelled, in spite
of their grossness. His hands were small. With
them, he worked over his hooded stove, and served
his customers, smiling with his mouth, that never
lighted his eyes in the same expression. His
thoughts were always emphatic, but his voice was
thin and high, a prayerful tenor that made him
sound bewildered. His most constant thought
about himself was that he needed to be hard. He
would shriek at high school boys who tried to
charge their cups of coffee and doughnuts. They
would smile, and walk out, and later pay him,
making him feel that some strength was missing
somewhere in him. But the air of steam hooting
softly above the range which he kept so well-shined

always restored his happiness, and he forgot the necessity of being as sceptical, as narrow-eyed, and as "hard" as the men of the town whom he knew as a fellow citizen. His pride lay in his Cafe, in the accomplishment of every small order with as much elegance as he could put into his cooking and serving.

That was why he had a waitress; it was, he said to himself, why in such disastrous times as these he still employed a waitress, though the crowds were thinned down to the old level of his early days, when he had been sufficient to cook and serve too. Every morning at seven o'clock, Mrs. Rocker arrived, and she stayed until ten at night, leaving Fat to close up at twelve. She went home to her naked boarded house that had one room and three beds for herself, her husband and their six children. Fat had called for her once in his car, to take her to work. The sight of the bed-clothes, the collapsing white enamel and brass beds, the hardened and shined and worn plaster of dirt on the floor, the happy, lousy children, the dogs and cats who slept and ate in the quilts and the dishes with the family, the smell of old lazy animals that filled the Rocker house, turned some-

thing in him to disgust and then pity. Mrs. Rocker
had been so cheerful always, so unexcited about
her way in life, that he'd assumed her to be well-
taken-care-of. After that, he couldn't pick her up,
and for weeks he struggled to be hard, and discharge her, for the place she came from must certainly threaten the cleanliness of his Cafe. But
if she saw his sullen agonies of intention that failed
to crystallize in act, she said nothing, but smiled
at him all day long, rubbing the counter with rags,
sweeping corners, pulling her hair out of her eyes,
and laughing through her lips that shielded very
few teeth. Fat remembered in despair the beautiful
girls who waited table in El Paso, with their eyes
painted blue and lashes black, their cheeks shading
from high crimson on the bone to plaster white
at the neck, their mouths rouged, their hair
bleached. He often comforted his soul in bed with
the scheme that he might one day marry such a
person and bring her to his bed and his Cafe. In
the meantime, Mrs. Rocker found things to do
all day long in the Cafe, smiling with trust upon
him, never questioning his rightness, and taking
her small wages from him with an agonizing, flat-
tering humility. She was simply dependent upon

him: and too, her husband, the children, the cats,
the bitch who trailed complacent dugs to feed the
litter for whose mother the Rockers could spare
a little out of even their own needs.

Yet as the months went past, and Spring approached, with no better trade, the grocery stock-
ing fewer dainties, the teachers staying home at
their boarding house when the County passed up
their salaries, Fat knew he must discharge Mrs.
Rocker, for there was nothing to pay her with.
He could do the work himself. It would be a relief.
In the afternoons, when great dinners should have
been mingling their rich fumes on his stove, with
Fat himself tasting and planning, the stir of spoon
in stinging messes, and deep content of filling up
kettles with most edible stews, he had lately been
sitting at the counter staring at newspaper pages,
not reading, only watching pictures, while he grew
drowsier and drowsier. The light changed and
ebbed from his long narrow Cafe, while the polished light brown of the counter vanished way
back in the room to shadow. The row of six tables
opposite the counter receded like a darkening
checkerboard. It would take a cup of coffee to
wake Fat up at four o'clock. Waking from his un-

sleepy daze, he would see Mrs. Rocker beyond the stove sitting on the packing box which was her own domain and smiling at him, as if she were waiting for him to awaken and take her smile. Fat thought angrily that she looked at him like an old fool hound dog bitch. But he could say nothing.

In the morning he went out to the grocery, and returned with a number of extras. Good times or bad, there was no difference to Mrs. Rocker. But he knew that the track meet would bring a lot of visitors, and he must be ready for them. He could take in enough to give Mrs. Rocker a week's wages and tell her not to come back. He had just spent every dime he owned in cash, and still owed the grocery. The morning was brisk and sunny. Mrs. Rocker left the door open to smell the wind off the plains, while she scrubbed at the large mirror facing the counter. Her cleaning stroke left rubs of light soap. Fat dumped his provisions on the table beside the range, and got hotly to work. Every time he turned around, she was smiling at him in the mirror, clouded and turned witch-like through the soapy reflection. His fat hands flew, shaking the upper arms. His skill revived; his knife flashed in the steamy sunlight around the stove. His spice boxes of green and red with gold exposition labels flourished above the copper pot and the rubbed aluminum vat where the soup bone protruded, boiled blank of succulence.

Presently Mrs. Rocker moved back of the counter. To pass Fat she had to squeeze against the counter, and he had to tiptoe and lean over the stove. It made him blush with exasperation. Who wanted her here anyway? She was in the way! She bent under the counter to get her sugar sack to refill the bowls. Her buttocks touched Fat behind his leg. He turned, ready with a fury that he couldn't explain. But Mrs. Rocker, innocently straightening up, moved down the counter at her work. She poured the sugar into the glass bowls with hinged metal tops. Fat said to himself with the emphasis of his opinion, "God damn it!" and went on working. Pretty soon, the old mood came on him again, and the mixture of his vapours, the ingenuities of his baking and his precision, satisfaction at applying the knowledge he had found out for himself and turned to use, let him begin to sing. His voice, so short of speaking, was expressive in song, and an original melody he had sung for years at his work, over and over, without change, rose from him and vanished up the tin hood of the cooking range, a sound like a part of the morning.

Later, Mrs. Rocker came back from the front of the Cafe and showed him an empty catsup bottle. Her expression assumed openly that it must be filled, and that Fat, who had everything so excellent, would see to it at once. He looked at her toothless smile, the dancing, familiar content of her blue eyes. Unable to name it, and so argue it away, he saw again his obligation to her, which he must meet or admit failure. How could he tell her there was no money at last? You don't buy catsup for nothing. Maybe tonight if there was a crowd in, there would be money for that. Also, money to send Mrs. Rocker away with.

She set the bottle down and went back up the aisle behind the counter. He felt again the severe need to be hard. It was not his fault that the Rockers would starve together, the old man, the kids, the cats and dogs, anything else that lived in that shack. He turned back to his stove. A rattling noise from the front of the Cafe made him turn. He threw down his butcher knife and shrieked with all of his confusion, dividing his small voice with his unfamiliar vehemence,

"Y' old fool, quit disturbing all that!"

Mrs. Rocker, who had been rearranging the Chesterfield cigarette cardboard displays, turned back to look at him, amazed and a little frightened. After staring at the sunlit window space, her eyes were dim until she was used to looking down the aisle of the Cafe. She saw, in a moment, that her fright was foolish. Fat was standing there, wiping his knife against his apron where it rounded across his stomach. He was smiling at her, his face was a heavy red, and the idea that he had sounded mad at her was lost in the new idea that he must have been joking, for he laughed a little before he turned to his meat block and began to slice chops.

In a few minutes the Sheriff came in for a cup of coffee. Mrs. Rocker served him, for that was her office; and when it was done, Fat strolled down the aisle and leaned on the counter where the Sheriff was, and the two men without speaking greeted each other by staring into each other's eyes, long and with unchanged looks on their faces, the Sheriff looking above his tilted cup and Fat leaning on his palm; neither having anything to say, yet mindful of the custom of sociability.

6.

COWARDS

IN THE ROAD CAMP EIGHT MILES FROM TOWN, LEO was awake when dawn began. He always woke up before sunrise, with a cold abandoned feeling in his stomach. He wrapped his thin arms around his chest, shivering at the fleshless articulation of himself, and watched the sky send reflections of light on the hazy brown earth. When the sun was up, the road camp would awaken. He would drink coffee, and thank the men for letting him sleep all night with them. Then he would start off again, walking on roadsides that had small stones in their dirt. When he stepped on a small stone, the jolt shocked by relay all the way up to his neck, and his head, a small head with white cheeks and reddish eyes, rolled with an ache. Cold and dismal though he felt the dawn to be, though it was early Spring and an occasional smell full of sweetness and promise touched his nose, he closed his eyes and inched into his blanket, planning in his mind how warm and happy it would be if he could stay all day, sleeping in the blanket in the little tent. But this was a positive desire; his strength, physical force and private will, was all gone. He hardly possessed opinions any more, saving only that one which let him believe in his heart that life was altogether miserable, a thing that could just as well be denied and ended, in spite of the strange gripings in his stomach that made him beg food every day, or in his mind that kept him toiling toward California, on alien roads in the company of no people but other aimless paupers like himself.

The sun now showed, after silent trumpetings of gold rays above the waving line of hills. A blur of gold that looked wet as melted metal grew along the horizon. An intimate light turned the sunward edges of all things in a brief golden beauty, cactus bushes, small pebbles, the poles of the telegraph by the road, the small tents of the camp, the barred and chained bodies of the trucks, any growth. Then the light became suddenly equal, and shadows faded, while a returned chill smote the air that had been briefly warmed. Distant hollows in the ground lost their blue mists of broken light, and clumps of trees came out from obscurity, and the town eight miles away in the sharp early light had a clean toy-like look.

Leo was fogging his memories in a returned sleep when the boy in the tent with him sat up with an explosion of breath, and a yawn full of noise like the sound a dog made when yawning. Leo's nerves sickened tight at the disturbance. His tent-mate crawled out into the light and went to wash. He was greeted by a dog. There was one more moment of stillness in which the humming of messages on the roadside wires travelled clear, and then the camp seemed all at once to be awake and busy. Cooking smells drifted to Leo's nose. The mucus wept a little at this stimulus, and roll-

ing his head with weak desire to arise, Leo felt
the saliva run down his mouth and choke him.
But he came to his crawling position, and left the
tent. His feebleness made him seem old, though
he was twenty-six. His smile of ingratiating thanks,
of willingness to help with anything, made him
look like a sneak, for a scar held one corner of his
mouth down, and any pleasant expression turned
to a sneer on his face, while in frown or repose his
face had a thin starved dignity, under the bald rise
of his round forehead that bulged and made his
head so much too big for his neck and shoulders.
The camp boss told him to sit down and wait for
breakfast, impatiently, embarrassed by the weak
murmur of Leo's voice, and the tragic affability
he so hardly managed.

At last, holding a tin cup of coffee that burned
his fingers, he knew a tide of courage run through
his aching tripes, and he told the men eating with
him that he was moving on to California that
day. He had been, he said, without work for fif-
teen months.

"In California I know plenty of people. I have
an uncle who is a lawyer. The climate will be
easier on me, too, than the East."

He spoke with a precision of word and tone, making reference to his past, which included education, ambition, content, and no plan for such a present as he owned. He told them he would make it in another week at the outside. From New Mexico to the coast was an easy route. The coffee, having shocked him into well-being, now cooled in him, and indigestion returned, his mood faltered, and he grew silent, weakened. The men ate stolidly, silent except to comment on cars that went by on the road, a few in series, then none for a long time. Leo looked after the cars.

"Damn their souls," he said.

The camp boss looked at him curiously.

"I had a car once," Leo continued, a pale flush showing on his cheekbones. It was a weak whimper that he made, and the boss indifferently turned back to his food, easily certain of what to think of cranks who magnified their hard luck into a whole attitude toward everybody else. But Leo went on talking, his big head shaking on its poor neck, making the only protest he knew to make against the circumstances of the life that let him lower every day into helplessness. It was a murmur, almost impersonal because of the feebleness of its delivery, against the larger lives that survived while his own faded. Everything he said referred to money, and its absence from his pockets. The men let him talk, hardly listening any more than if they were listening to the crying of a cat. Nor did Leo expect them to listen, for he was talking to himself. It was a rehearsal of the thoughts that made him dream at night. He presently fell silent, knowing no conviction from his breakfast or his tirade.

The men got up. The cook watched them dump their dishes into the big tub for washing. They went to the trucks, and soon a wild firing of the exhausts sounded out. The trucks lined up on the road heading east. The boss told Leo he was sorry he couldn't offer a lift on the road but the trucks were all working in the opposite way. Leo said it was all right; he thanked the boss for the night's shelter and the breakfast. The affability in his eyes touched the older man, and as Leo turned to walk off to California, stumbling slightly on the rutty roadside, the boss had a feeling of pity and half-comprehension, which if he could have said it would have told that every scale in life had eagerness to exist, and that to see this eagerness blanched by forces beyond control was pitiable.

Walking slowly, Leo had travelled over a mile when a car pulled up beside him. It was already hot in the open country, and the sparse sweat that his body could produce showed on his face. The man in the car said that a man he knew, the road camp boss, had told him to pick up this guy. Leo got into the car, breathing through his mouth. He smiled his unalterable sneer, and settled back on the seat. The driver was a fellow about thirty-five or so, Leo thought, heavily tanned, and thickly built. He was smoking a pipe. His face was bland and almost merry. The car was an old coupe, travelling with loud winds of mechanical maladjustment. Yet it was cool in the car, and Leo felt a kindness toward the day that brought a sensation of strength with it.

His driver said he was coming down from his filling station in the hills to town, and could take Leo as far as that. He claimed to be always willing to give a guy a lift. He spoke with a Southern accent, and presently revealed that he was from Georgia, and in a rush of confidence that surprised Leo, he sketched his past with an assurance that it must be of interest to anyone. He'd been in the navy during the War, and after that had a job with a bank that didn't pay enough, and it

was a raise to drive a long-haul freight truck in
Alabama. That didn't last very long. The Texas
oil fields looked good, and when they cut down,
he drifted up to New Mexico and got a job helping in this filling station. He enjoyed talking about
himself, contented with his past, and requiring
very little of the present. Leo thought him an en-
viable person, for the bodily strength he had, and
because life to Leo had become the necessity of
wanting what others had. Facts about Leo didn't
interest the driver. He gave no time for any con-
fession. The first interruption in his agreeable rem-
iniscing was a blowout. The left rear tire gave
out, and the rocking car slid on loose gravel for
several yards before it was halted. The driver sat
still for a moment, humorously nodding his head.

"Wul, Gawd da-yum!" he said.

Then he shrugged, and got out, lazily, stretching his arms after tucking his pipe away. He
knocked the seat cushion out of place, and dragged
out the oily dusted tools. Leo stood by him, wanting to help. The driver threw him a wrench to
start loosening the nuts on the rim, while he himself jacked up the axle. Leo set the head of the
wrench over a hexagonal nut, and threw the force

of his body against the lever's force. Up his arms
went pains with a fluid swiftness. He smiled and
tried again. A little gray caked dirt fluttered to
the ground from the wrench head. He couldn't
turn it. His chest began to hurt. He coughed, slak-
ing his dry mouth. In a moment, the driver came
around beside him, and then saw that nothing
had been done, he grasped Leo's arm with a lifting grab and set him aside, making an impatient
and scornful disposal of such a puny wretch. Leo
stood by. Rage boiled in his throat. In a few
twists of the wrench and an easy slide of muscles,
the driver had the nuts off the wheel, and the tire
bouncing on the ground as he leaned it against
the running board. While he worked, the driver
whistled a tune. Now and then he looked at Leo,
who was sitting on the shady side of the car. He
thought Leo was laughing until he saw that it was
shivering that made his head wobble and his shoulders tremble. But there was nothing to shiver
about, and he ignored it, turning back to the new
tire which he was screwing to the wheel.

Leo was shivering from injustice. His arm was
bruised where the thin flesh had been rubbed
against the bone by this man who had set him aside

like so much tumbleweed. In his heart was a
need to refuse further help from such a man. He
stood up. The driver began to let the jack down.
The car settled on to the new tire and the driver
withdrew the jack. Leo watched the spare tire
flatten down almost as low as the punctured tire
had been. He waited for the driver to see this.
He pointed it out to him, smiling with a timid
return of friendliness. The scarred lip showed his
teeth. It looked like a sneer, a delight in this
foolish hard luck. The driver looked at the tire.
He kicked it. He turned back to Leo and said, in
a roar of sudden exasperation,

"Well, wipe off that God damn smile!"

He went to the front of the car and pulled out
an old tire pump, and set to work. It was slow
going, and the tire rose imperceptibly. Leo sat
watching a negro approaching them from down
the road. Making a small cloud of dust with his
kicking feet and swinging his hips from side to
side as he walked, a mincing, muscular stride, the
negro approached, and Leo could see that he was
young, and of medium height. His eyes were
sleepy. He was smiling. In his hand he carried an
old stick. The driver didn't see him coming, but
when the negro said,

"Mownin' boss,"
he turned, resting his fist on the pump handle.

"Whey you come f'om, nigga," said the driver, in an exaggerated accent that Leo coupled with the fact that he was from Georgia.

"F'm down de road," said the negro, leaning in a friendly way against the rear of the car. "Havin' tah trouble?"

"Git a holt hah," said the driver, throwing the pump handle toward the negro, who smiled like a pickaninny with candy and did nothing. The driver tightened his stance on his spread legs. He looked at the negro waiting. The negro laughed out merrily, full of sunshine and goodwill on the morning when the wind blew so gently and so freshly. He crossed his legs, standing with a certain natural elegance, a racial and physical ability to express his mood with every change of his body.

"Did'n yoh hah me, nigga?" said the driver. Leo saw that his face was a deep plum red. His own mouth turned dry, suddenly, when he saw that the driver was angry. The negro closed his eyes and shook his head, shaggywise, spilling out the mood of comic happiness he held.

"No zah, boss," he said in a rich voice, hoarse with comedy. "Ah don' want pump no tahs

. . . ," exploding into a hooting laugh that assumed universal amusement at the situation. Leo
saw the red fade from the neck and head of the
driver, and relaxed thinking that his anger was
gone. But stooping quickly to the ground, the
driver picked up in each hand a small stone that
would fit the closed fist, and with a blast of breath
from his nostrils, he bounded forward and hit the
negro twice, once with each fist, against the temple
and on the jaw. The negro's eyes fell open, and
he choked on his laughter. He dropped his stick.
He fell against the car and rubbed his head. In
his hoarse voice, roughened first by amusement, he
began to wail, making no words, but only doleful
syllables. Before him stood the driver, boxing the
air, and leaning and leaning with his body, and
smiling with the simplest face of pleasure. There
wasn't the slightest look of fury about him now.
His merry eyes were lighted with fun. The rhyth-
mic, slow spar of his hands had a gaiety in them
that was full of grace. He turned his body at the
waist, swinging rapidly. He waited for the negro
to recover his breath, and to lose his amazement
of pain.

The negro lowered his hands from his head,

with his enormous fingers spread out. Leo thought it was like a monkey in a zoo lowering his paws from his puzzled head when he had a headache, a thing he couldn't explain or touch, some alien menace.

"Come ohn," said the driver. His voice was teasing and humorous. "Hit me: hit me, nigga."

He backed off as the negro lunged forward on his feet. Blood was curling down the negro's face from the cut temple. He shook his head. The driver poked out with one rapid arm, and cuffed the negro's ear, a stinging and taunting hit. Leo sat down on the running board suddenly, too shaken to stand. He tasted the coffee from breakfast as it regurgitated into his throat. He swallowed with control. The negro was weakened by astonishment. Leo clenched his mouth and hoped the negro would hit the driver.

"Hit him!" screamed Leo suddenly.

"Ah'll hit 'im," said the driver, lazily looking at Leo with appreciation, and instantly thrust his fist into the negro's belly. The whimpering stopped. The negro took in a series of shocked little breaths through his mouth, making a sound. Then he skipped out from his position against the rear of the car, and dancing wildly on the road, he gave an appearance of having his tail erect, with his head up and his back curved in. His hands played across his front. The driver glowing with delight danced around as the negro's eyes cleared and watched for an opening. It came, and the black hands drove to the pink jaw, that jerked away. It was the last blow the negro landed.

"Oh, yeah?" said the driver, and clutching his stones till his palms sweated against them, he swung right and left against the negro's head, his body; breaking the left ear and ripping teeth down into the bone with a remote crackling sound. He beat the negro back to the side of the road. The stoned fists cracked against the black skull. They drove into the negro's belly, rising up under the heart and the ribs. Leo saw the negro stagger and fall into the ditch, and ran forward from horror. The driver leaped down into the low ditch beside the road and picked the negro up. He stood him on his swaying legs, and knocked up the negro's arms, making an insolent demand that the negro defend himself, guard his body before the new attack. Blood ran down from the negro's eye, looking pink upon the grayed flesh of the face. The driver grinned. His pink jaws were widened by the pleasure of his blows. The pain of the negro's first blow on his face was something exciting and stirring, like the quickest delight imaginable. The negro wandered in tiny circles, hardly standing. Along with the sedate and narrow welling of blood out from his lips came a whispered wail. The driver leaped once more. He drove one hand to the negro's mouth, closing the fat lips and whitening them. He struck with a wet accurate sound at the jaw with the other hand. The negro's eyes rolled upward, and the lids stayed open, and the eyes showed white. Bleeding slowly, the negro fell to the ground in the ditch, where it was half shady. His breath wheezed with wetness. The driver threw down the small stones from his hands and spat on the ground. He looked cheerful. He stirred the negro once with his foot, almost gently, and watched for any awakening. There was none. Scratching himself in the crotch with an easing sensation of triumph, he went back to the car and slapped Leo on the shoulder.

"Ol' nigga get fresh wid me," he said with a certain tender simplicity. He laughed softly in his throat, and leaned down and picked up the brass tire pump. He bent his back up and down over the pump. The tire rose slowly again.

Leo went to the side of the ditch and looked in. Half in sunlight, the beaten man lay like a large baby, his knees bent, his forearms bent back and the hands lying with relaxed curled fingers above his shoulders. His head was rolled to one side, and the red and white issue from the mouth flowed slackly to the ground. The eyes looked dead. But threads of tortured reflex tightened in the body, and it quivered every few seconds, accompanied by a windy grunt from the working throat of the negro.

Leo sat on the edge of the ditch and wept. He could taste his own illness in his mouth. He wept without ideas and forgetful of words. In his weeping were flashes like blindness that showed him how much he hated the driver and his acts. He felt hatred for himself, who had stood vomiting and helpless while the negro had been beaten down to a ditch. He saw the body stir now, slowly, as if awakening from some hibernation. But it quieted again at once, with only the shocking quiver tightening and loosening in the torso and along the legs.

The driver threw down the pump and kicked the tire.

"'At's O.K.," he called to Leo. He unscrewed the pump hose from the tire valve, and threw the pump into the seat with the other tools. He replaced the seat cushion. Then he walked over to the ditch. He chuckled, and said as if he liked the negro,

"Ol' nigga be 'bout an hou' comin' 'roun. . . ."

Leo set his wrists against his eyes to stop his weeping. He stood up.

"Time we got goin'," said the driver, and turned back to the car.

"You're going to leave him here?" said Leo.

The driver stopped. He laughed generously.

"Fo' Chras' sake!" he said, and then disdained further answer or comment. He clambered into the car and started the engine. He called to Leo to hurry. Looking again, Leo saw the negro there, whose life slowed in the black body. Then taken by a strange panic in himself, Leo turned and ran to the car and clattered in beside the driver. They drove off. The wind cooled them. Nothing could cool the burning shame Leo felt, to be riding here now. The driver lighted his pipe and sighed, for his body was contented with the spend of violence it had made. He smiled dreamily. His mouth moved around the stem of his pipe as he talked.

"Ol' nigga," he said, with amusement. "He sho' made a mistake to git fresh wid me! Eh?"

He turned to Leo.

"He sure did," said Leo, loathing himself.

"Sure beat up on 'im, didn' I?"

"I'll say," said Leo.

"See 'im try to hit me?"

"Yeah," said Leo, and laughed. The droll pity in his voice satisfied the driver. Its cowardice set Leo trembling in his breast. He closed his eyes, looking inward upon himself. All he saw was a tired soul, begging sleep.

7.

UNDER THE WIND

THE COURTHOUSE STOOD IN THE HOT SUNLIGHT, with shadows of the tall trees washing over its yellow brick front. The building was two stories high, rising toward a roof of chocolate coloured slate. In front was a tower that rose a third story, and ended bluntly, in a cluster of dormered windows. All the windows of the building were tall and narrow, with rounded tops. Their edges were trimmed in gray stone. The window woodwork and the doorways, the glimpse of cool hallway inside, were finished in dark varnish, brown with a glow of red beneath. The Courthouse rising from a country of dust, had something of dust's colour in all its parts, except where the shadows waved like a cool wash across its front, in blue leaf echoes. The trees were great cottonwoods, planted forty years before, watered in their early sprouting by the ditch that used to flow from the river; grown in their middle years to be large enough for hangings after posses returned with human trophy; now stately, like patriarchs whose wisdom lives in their mere physical presence, after all sight and mind have been feebled.

On the thin scatterings of grass before the Courthouse, the crowd grew as the morning went on. Shortly after eight they had begun to assemble, leaving their cars, trucks and coupes and sedans, touring cars, around the corner and down the main street, parked in front of the newspaper office and Fat's Cafe, a line of various cars spreading as far as the garage at the point where Main street became highway. They came with lunches wrapped in paper. They came with empty stomachs and fearful breasts. Their greetings were lively and happy, as the eddies in the crowd changed and distributed the individuals. Coming together for a common purpose, the people of the town and the country were easy in their meeting, like people who have for generations drawn comfort from the camp meetings and revivals of the plains. They made a texture of gossip, walking and glancing at the Courthouse under the trees. High in the yellow green boughs the wind turned coolly.

From the throng rose a sound, broken yet sustained and overlapped, like a murmur of bees, heard closely. They talked about the troubles that touched them all equally, in common. There was no money and since there was no money, often there was no food, and certainly no good clothes. As individuals talked, their private and separate prides appeared, and though they had come like everyone else to demand and receive help from the Government this morning, their eyes and their voices carried hints from the past, when the ranges were cropped by great roving herds of cows that moved like the mottled shadows of clouds over the tawny unchanging land, and money rolled into the bank in town; when the stock corrals at Ramona, painted white at the railroad side, were

always full of the rich herds waiting to be pulled
East to market; when there was a vast cotton market waiting to buy the white blooms from the local
fields; when oil was predicted between here and
Ramona, and the drilling crews came, setting up
derricks that worked all night, with great white
lamps flaring so they could be seen for miles. . . .
A past unmindful of hope, for the great plenty and
occupation of its time.

Now in the morning that grew hotter as they
waited, stirring uneasily because it was after ten
and nothing was done yet, the gossip enlarged
itself from mouth to mouth. It was true that the
representatives of the Government had arrived
from Ramona a little after eight, coming by the
seven-forty-five express from the North. They were
seen in the Courthouse, going over the files of the
local emergency committee with the Sheriff. In
the meantime, the rumour grew. The Government
had sent money in bags. There was food in boxes
inside the Courthouse, held safe in the vault,
where the gold was, in its bags, a safe enough place
since the bank had failed. A thin girl with a prominent breastbone, and excited eyes with a wry light
in them, moved forward through the crowd, hold-

ing by the hand a tall heavy man who grinned fool-
ishly at being dragged along so. Her voice was
shrill, telling anyone that it was time to get help
from the Government, and that it was also easy,
with the gold in the Courthouse vault that had
been moved in during the night, for safety.

"Did you hear that?" exclaimed a heavy old
woman who sat on a bench near the front steps
of the Courthouse. "They brought gold in during
the night, in the Courthouse, during the night,
they was attacked during the day, so they brought
it during the night."

The news roved and crackled through the people, several hundred of them.

The door of the Courthouse was open, and they
could see the dark hallway running the whole
depth of the building, a brown tunnel with cool
light at its far end. Now and then a door would
open in the corridor, and a clerk would walk across
to another office. Each of these small events caused
the crowd to stir and shift, pressing closer. The
people in front thought the people behind were
crowding them toward the building, leaving plenty
of space back there near Main street. But the
space near Main street was filling gradually, as

more people came. Old men and women grew
tired, and their limbs began to tremble. They
sweated and wiped their faces. At the far edge
of the crowd, a small man with a heavy head on
a thin neck lifted himself on tiptoe and craned
for a look at the Courthouse door. He could see
nothing. Slowly, with heavy breathing, he began
to slide his way through the crowd. His voice,
begging passage, was high, a whine, like a cat's.

At the front of the throng, a little girl, tired of
waiting, ran up the steps and into the door. The
crowd laughed, seeing their own desires so frankly
acted out for them. An inner door opened, and a
strange man led the child back to the sunlight,
smiling with an official frown at the crowd. He
stepped back in the building and closed the doors.
The little girl began to cry, from petulance. The
crowd was silent, totally, a hush like the air in
the treetops. Then sounds broke, they let their
opinions out, and the press of each person upon
the next, the hot morning, the desperation of
their needs came together and lifted the sounds of
voices into a low menace. Suddenly the bodies were
pushed together. A witless agreement made everyone surge toward the doorway. The old woman

sitting on her bench near the steps was overturned. The bench broke down, and she cried out in distress. Her son was somewhere else in the crowd, and her husband had been talking to a tall old man under the far tree. The people stopped and helped the old woman to her feet. They set the bench up again. Someone cried out, "Stop pushing!" and the tension relaxed. They breathed apart again. Perplexity grew, wondering what in the world could be going on in the Courthouse. A young boy, bright with eagerness, ran to the trunk of the tallest cottonwood, and clamping it with his arms and knees, he climbed up. He walked out on the heavy branches toward the windows in the front of the building. He laughingly peered down, and the crowd looked up at him, delighted with his audacity, the scheme for seeing what was going on inside. He sat down on the bough and swung his legs.

"Can't see a thing," he called.

The old woman on the broken bench looked up and saw her son. She cried out to him to come down. He laughed. He turned and ran back along the bough, balancing with his brown arms outstretched, running on his toes, his yellow head

bent to avoid the small branches about him. The
leaves shivered at the impact of his feet on the
bough. When he came to the trunk, he reached
up for a higher branch and swung on it with his
hands. He turned his body in midswing, and
hooked his legs over the branch. Then lazily he
swung himself up to a sitting position there and
sat looking down on the crowd which had forgotten him. He was panting; his pink breast rose
and fell under his rough blue shirt. He was
thoughtless and contented with muscular play.

Shortly before eleven, Do Miller drove into
town from Ramona, where he had been to pick
up a part for a car he was repairing in his High
Way Garage. The street choked with cars surprised him, but he remembered the meeting, treat-
ing it mentally with great scepticism, having heard
at Ramona that the Government people were coming down just to make a survey, and see what
had to be done, and how to do it. He drove his
service truck as near the Courthouse as he could,
and then walked half a block to see what was going
on. He saw the crowd, stirring in the heat of approaching noon. Nothing seemed to be going on.
It was sure a big crowd. Most everybody in town

was there. He recognized dozens of people. He laughed at the expression made by the backside view of the fat man on the outskirts of the crowd, who was dancing on tiptoe, with his dimpled arms raised, in airy efforts to grow tall enough and light enough to see through the crowd, or above it. Do Miller rubbed his forehead with the back of his hand, habitually mindful of the motor grease that might be on his fingers, and turned away. The spider gear he had got needed installation. So far as he could see, there was just a mob of people waiting there for nothing. Touched by his own vague approaches to philosophy, he swelled his chest. Then he felt sorry that so many people would be disappointed if the Government people really had nothing to give them. He drove his truck back to the High Way Garage and went to work.

In the cool stucco interior of his garage, after a while, he could hear the noise. He sat back on his heels, setting his wrists on his knees, to keep the greasy touch of his hands off. In the whole stillness of the day, with the town deserted in favour of the meeting, no cars moving, or bodies passing, the noise grew and expended itself without stop-

ping. The crowd was yelling. Do walked to the
open double doors of the garage and looked down
the street. He could see nothing. But the sound
was angrier, and his mind made sudden pictures
for him of who was yelling, the people he knew
so well. He couldn't picture Andrew Lark screaming at a blank building, or Mrs. Vosz or old Fat.
Mrs. Rood, whose car he had sold for her for six-
teen dollars, would not raise her voice like that.
Mrs. Lark was a proper little old woman, with the
most modest eyes he had ever seen, always down-
cast, except when she said something fooling,
when they were raised for a sly look. He threw
down his tools and stuck his pipe in his mouth.
He started to walk back toward the Courthouse
plaza. In his middle was a slightly sick feeling,
for the unrecognizable sort of noise the crowd
was making. He thought he could begin to hear
words, the closer he got. But they just eluded his
ear that would sort them out of the confusion.
When he climbed on top of one of the battered
trucks driven in by a farmer, he saw the waving
arms, the shaking heads that roused the howls.
He stood in the sunlight, which was almost straight
above him, intense and palpable.

Suddenly the noise from the crowd lowered.

A softer sound, the panting of all the breaths, made an expectant pause. The door of the Courthouse shook in someone's grasp again, and then it opened. The double doors were thrown open. The crowd slacked off a little. Air spaces widened between the figures. On the stoop of the entrance, the Sheriff appeared. Someone called out his name, and he waved his arm, genially, yet his face was cross. He rested his hand on his hip and slouched one leg. His voice was hardly audible, yet it was firm and impatient.

"We are doin' the best we can in here. It wasn't our idea to have any mass meetin', anyway."

Someone called to him, "Cheer up, Sheriff!" and the crowd laughed, nervously. They didn't know what his words meant. He opened his mouth as if to speak again, but changed his mind, and looked across the faces once or twice, and then backed into the doorway, which he left open.

From the rear of the crowd down to the very front, wriggling his way and panting, touching people's necks with his wet cold hands to make them give way, Leo struggled forward. He was possessed by a desire to be a part of the crowd.

When they murmured, now, at being abandoned
again by the Sheriff, he lifted his voice with theirs,
making no words, but only a dutiful meow of
menace that was absentminded, bent as he was
on reaching the front row of the impatiently waiting people. He knew no one around him. The
driver had left him at the edge of town, hours
earlier. Leo wanted to be washed; he felt that some
atonement must be done by him before he could
be again a human being, after the events of the
early morning on the roadside. He let himself into
activity, instead of thought. He crawled against the
resistant bodies of the crowd, trying to pass them
and be one of them. His face was white and his
eyes fired with exhaustion.

On the outside of the throng, Fat rose again
on tiptoe, keeping his balance by lifting his arms.
He could see nothing. But in a moment he heard
a sigh go up, some greeting, and knew that the
people were busy with something. He became
suddenly angry at being so ineffectual. He felt,
in a quick minute of recognition, the core of something hard in him at last. With a fury like pleasure, he began to beat his way forward, not caring
for his neighbors, and determined to find out why
nothing was done for a starving country.

Down on her bench, Mrs. Vosz settled her arms on her bosom. She looked up to the stoop, and nodded her head with a vague matriarchal dignity. In the doorway, pausing briefly, was a strange man, who smiled at the crowd, and then walked slowly forward to the top step. He was followed by the Sheriff and another man and a woman who was taller than any of the men. She was dressed in a blue linen suit. She wore glasses and turned her head from side to side, smiling with her upper teeth exposed. The crowd made sounds of expectancy, and satisfaction. They turned to each other, saying, "Well, at last." The Sheriff lifted his hand, and indicating the first stranger, he said,

"This is Major Drew, and he will say a few words to you."

Drew smiled to the Sheriff, and bowed, with a platform courtesy that seemed out of place. He turned to the crowd, and raised his shoulders and dropped them, settling his arms behind his back like an orator. He lifted his neck out of its collar a little, and cleared his voice. He had a large pink head and raised eyebrows. When he talked, they couldn't hear his voice at the rear of the crowd. He said that he and Mr. Edwards and Miss Molton had made a preliminary survey of the

needs in this county. So far as was possible, they
had read every report of complaint and request
filed in the Courthouse. Maybe he should explain,
said Major Drew, that the Government, in these
matters, always required a preliminary survey,
which was to be followed by a routine relief agency,
where food and clothing would be issued as needed.
He hoped it would be possible to establish this
agency here within a month. In the meantime,
he wished to say that the interest exhibited in
the work was very gratifying.

Major Drew paused and brought his hands
around from resting on his rump. He folded them
in front, and cracked the knuckles, stretching his
arms downward.

Miss Molton glimmered with her glasses and her
teeth at the crowd. The blood was pounding in her
throat, and her mouth was dry. Her smile was a
twist of strain on her face, for she watched the
crowd, and their quietness was strangely terrifying. Major Drew looked at her for understanding.
The crowd had listened, but said nothing, and
seemed to understand nothing. They simply stood,
waiting, in the dusty heat of noon, under a some-
what risen wind flying faster over the low buildings
of the town.

Major Drew nodded his head paternally at the near members of the crowd, and began to speak again.

"We find that your conditions here are very uncomfortable, of course," he said. "It will be our aim to bring help as soon as we can. But I *will* say, I *must* say, that up in the northern counties, the suffering is far worse than yours here is. We have been working night and day, nigh-tan-dday, up there."

"When do we get ours!" cried a voice from the crowd.

The crowd let itself down with a noise like wind. Here it was, the question, at last. Many voices brought it up, now, and full of self-pity, some of the old people began to moan and weep, holding forth their thin arms where the bones showed against the skin like the stems in a leaf, waving their arms vaguely at the group on the steps. Major Drew stepped back a pace and then forward again, as if he had made a mistake to retreat. He extended his arms.

"Please, please," he said. "Let me explain."

The news travelled back through the crowd to the rear, which had not heard, that the relief agency was a lie. There was no help. They talked

about investigating and reporting, and so on. As it
passed from unminded mouth to angry ear, the
news lost all reality, and became merely something to defy. Knowing hunger, and remembering
a winter of sharp helplessness, the people heard
rumours inside themselves as clearly as they did
the words from the steps.

   Miss Molton was talking now. Her voice was
piercing, and every ear could hear. Her words
trembled from the strain of her sincerity. Her
tongue clove to her mouth from nervousness. It
made her sound guilty, and the crowd hated her
for her hesitations. She told them that when the
relief station was opened, it would run as long as
it was needed, with herself in charge. She said she
was sorry that the news had leaked out that the
officials would be here today, because they were
not prepared for any meeting, or to give out any
food. Or money. Whatever had brought them together, she was glad she had a chance now.

   "I'm glad I have a chance now," she said, wring-
ing her bony hands upon her breast, "because I
want a chance to tell you all how much everybody
understands how brave you all have been in these
hard times and they have been hard, and they

might go on being hard times for a little while longer, and, but, the idea is that we have all got to do our best for each other. So now that we understand the situation and all about how it is here, why, Major Drew and Mr. Edwards and myself, we are all going to see that things, your problems and things here, will be taken care of. As soon as possible. The very first minute."

She opened her mouth to say something again, but she had no saliva, and she swallowed painfully. A bright wetness stood in her eyes, from the strain of speaking against the will of the crowd, that now crept forward thoughtlessly, its faces strained and blanked by the effort to realize the fact that there was no relief about to be given out. There was no gold in the bags in the Courthouse vault, or trucks of food. Miss Molton coughed, and then turned abruptly back to Major Drew and Mr. Edwards.

The atmosphere over the plaza seemed to grow closer and hotter. A mood like the warming of the way ran over the heads. For a moment, a bated interval, there was nothing. And then on a wail, a woman's voice rose, screaming,

"We want money!"

"—food!" declared another voice.

They had stood most of the morning, waiting.

Without a summons, they had gathered from all their places to come, and once together, to receive.

They awaited leadership. They stirred from foot to foot, imploring one another with blank eyes.

The wind, like something in that human weather before the building, sang dismally against the trees, and the air darkened a faint little as the fine dust of the surface was stirred and turned.

The voices were talking against one another, yet with the same burden behind them. The relief committee on the stoop could not be heard. They nodded, with pleading expressions on their faces. They shook hands with the crowd in pantomime, and failed to believe that a temper was gathering into a unanimous strength. To look at them, the people were kind and honest, average. Already one or two at the outskirts were beginning to drift away toward the waiting cars. Miss Molton nodded to her companions, and they turned. They went into the building. The Sheriff stared at the way the crowd fell back upon itself as the doors swung shut. Then he heard the wave begin to rise.

The mob tightened instantly. Small eddies of people in parts of the crowd turned against itself. In one of them, Heart DeLancy began to shriek an address at her immediate neighbors. She worked until her arms were free of the pressing people, and then above her head she waved them like brands. Her words tumbled out in a shrill line, and Rolf Kunkel, standing behind her, pressing upon her in a public intimacy that flushed his veins, heard a mad eloquence stream from her. Heart was wild in his eyes. Her strength was amazing. As she turned to free her message of discontent and desire, she struck him on the shoulder with her arm, and the blow hurt with a dull energy. It enflamed him to see her staring at him and screaming, as if she hardly knew him, yet had to convince him. She was convincing others. The crowd settled close around her, waving their arms. They called out agreements with her. There was gold in the vault, and it might as well help lives now as later.

She turned and pointed to the door of the Courthouse. There was a low silence, while the crowd paused, and the voice of an old man rose up saying a prayer. Awed and happy, the crowd knew its strength. They began to sway slightly, and Mrs.

Vosz's famous contralto voice was lifted in a line of
song. Under the tallest cottonwood, Ellen Rood
heard herself singing also, a pale troubled voice
that came back to her ears with all the force of
her despairs that she had never yet yielded to, as
she was yielding now. The old man praying was
Andrew Lark. Every sentence he spoke ended on
a rising inflection. His eyes were closed, and he
was trembling, transported out of himself.

It was a short pause, filled with the breath of
exaltation. Heart cried out again. There were
echoes. They began to push against the bodies of
each other, and as they moved, together, their
voices roared. They started across the sidewalk to
the foot of the steps. Leo was turned and rolled
like a log in the current, rubbed against the trunk
of one of the great trees.

"Oh Lord?" declared Andrew Lark, "where
Thy steps take us, so there shall we walk? Lord.
Amen: amen? Oh, Thy steps, Lord? We shall walk
in Thy ways? Glory?"

As she murmured a faint melody, vague and
hopeful, Ellen Rood admitted a strange peaceful-
ness to her breast. Her heart seemed to be over-
flowing with richness, for she was at one with the

people around her, and she remembered the re-
vival times when the bleak sorrows of her little
family had been made to glow with some fine life
in the flood of prayer. So she felt now, clasping
and unclasping her fingers; her eyes stared and her
voice trailed uncertainly in the wake of her joy.
It was escape. She was forgetful of herself, her
children, the dangers of the morning, and the
emptiness of the future. The crowd around her
were moving and tightening toward the Courthouse. She raised her arms and imitated the
threatening gestures of those around her. Her face
was changed. She would not have known herself.

Mrs. Vosz struggled to her feet as the crowd
closed about the bench where she'd been sitting
all morning. The fervour of old Andrew Lark's
prayer had started her singing, and she could see
his face, tilted back and free to the windy sunlight.
The slyness was gone from his leathery wrinkles.
His eyes were dropped half shut, and he prayed
with his mouth slacked, biting no labial words,
only letting his tongue articulate in his mouth.
Except for the dim movement of the tongue, he
looked like a man dead, whitened by sun and
sightless. His voice continued with a curious power.

Mrs. Vosz began to weep at the beauty of her
singing, which rose and fell in a mournful strident
sound, hollow of music but charged with meaning
for the crowd.

Heart DeLancy was steady in her effort. So much
in her was being fused to a purpose that her influence travelled through the crowd. At one point
she saw Leo fixed upon her with his immense eyes,
and in a recognition that belonged to the genius
of the moment, she knew his hysterical strength,
and she grasped his thin hand over the heads of
those near, and burning with a power that de-
pleted itself only in action, they cried out and
charged forward, making shocks and impulses that
bruited from body to body and mind to mind.
They moved. The singing of the women, the
prayers from the old men were submerged.

Do Miller had about decided to go back to the
garage when he saw the crowd tighten and heard
the praying voices rise. He laughed to himself, at
the inappropriateness of the sounds. He was moved
again by the peculiar feeling that people he knew
well, every day, seemed now like strangers, as parts
of the crowd. He saw little old Mrs. Lark biting
her lips together with an expression like a taste of

vinegar, and beating her fists against the air, as she shuffled forward with the mob. With a red face oiling itself in sweat, Fat, the proprietor of the Cafe, had beaten his way through the crowd and now stood looking with an expression of stern virtue over all the heads near him. Do was simply conscious of the changes he saw. There was a shock through the crowd, some physical tug like the pull that goes down the line in a freight train from car to car. The crowd started up the steps, and at the same moment a loose stone sailed through the air and wrecked a window in the left wing of the front door. Do Miller jumped up again on the truck where he'd stood watching before. The glass chimed to the stone stoop. Men began scrambling on the ground for loose dirt and rock to hurl. Heart found a brick bat and threw it. It struck the stone trim of a window and fell feebly. They engulfed the steps.

The doors opened quickly.

The Sheriff stepped out holding his gun. With his left arm he motioned the crowd back, frowning sickly. These were his townsmen. He raised his arm over the charging mass. He fired three shots in the air, at random, and a few clipped fresh

leaves spiraled slowly down from the cottonwoods.
The three shots broke the noise with silence. The
people stopped.

When the silence was complete, the Sheriff said,
"I'm sorry to use a gun against all my friends.
Now quit, and get home out of here. We've had it
hard all year, and 'tain't any easier right now. But
it's going to be, soon's possible. They ain't any
gold in here, nor food, nor the like. We can man-
age for another two weeks. Now we got to hold on.
Now break it up."

He watched in silence then until he saw the first
falter in the crowd. The sound of his three shots,
fired over their heads into the air, seemed still to
echo. Someone sobbed once, with fright and
fatigue. It made a sound suggestive of shame. The
crowd loosened. Some shook their heads. They
returned as if from a dream to the direction of
their ways, the separate lives that had been so in-
tensely merged and shared.

With a scowl of friendly approval, the Sheriff
nodded, and turned back into the building, leaving the door open, the way unprotected, for he
knew by feeling that the menace was relaxed. The
people moved out to the street from under the
shade of the great trees, breaking up into small

groups for talk, reassuring one another, and divided between shame and indignation at having been fired upon. They found their cars. How much longer they would be able to buy or barter gasoline and so keep the ability to move from farm to town, they could not know.

From behind the Courthouse, they saw the Sheriff's car appear with the Government officials in it, heading toward Ramona to catch the afternoon train.

Mrs. Vosz stood by her bench waiting for Franz and Mr. Vosz to get her. She was weak from the excitement of the day, and the tears still rolled down her cheeks from the commotion that her singing, her yielding, had made in her. She saw the crowd thinning. They stirred the dust. The wind picked up the dust and made a dull gold haze in the air. She saw Mr. Vosz moving toward her slowly; his sober stride contracted her emotions. She knew how he hated fuss. She wiped her eyes with her shiny fat wrists, and pressed her bosom to find control. She began to smile for him, when someone screamed

"Look!"

and she turned to see.

Among the branches of the tallest cottonwood

there was a slow rustle. She saw two swinging legs
appear below the bottom branch, and then the fall
of a body, that rolled on the dust and fought
against stillness by cramping its knees upward. She
saw the face of her boy Franz smiling with absentminded pain. On the white breast through the
blue shirt she saw a well of scarlet. The remnant
of the crowd closed about him. She fancied she
heard him call her. Whenever she needed it most,
strength came up in her. She gave the back of the
bench a shove for impetus, and walked with a violent weighty stride to the shade of the tall tree. The
people opened for her. She knelt down with gasps
of effort for her immense fat legs and body. She
gathered Franz delicately into her arms and tried
for his pulse. She had no tears, and she knew from
the blue veil of his eyelids, the whiteness of his
mouth and the inertia of his body that he was badly
hurt.

"It must have been the shot," said someone in
the crowd. "He fired them into the trees."

Franz opened his eyes and with an ashamed
gallantry at his succumbing, he nodded and smiled
that this was so. They saw the flesh eaten from
his palms by the bark of the tree, where he had

clutched them to keep from falling at once. His
face was scratched by twigs and little branches.
The blood rolled out of his breast and sopped the
handkerchief his mother was holding against him.
Mr. Vosz was suddenly beside her. In a low voice
she ordered him to back the car into the plaza.
People drifted close shaking their heads, and a new
resentment against the Sheriff arose. Trembling,
Mr. Vosz got into his car. Franz was dying, he
could see it. How could his mother bear up so!
They lifted the boy into the car. Fat had run to
his Cafe across the street for clean napkins. They
made bandages. Mrs. Vosz saw in her mind a surge,
a threat of all that this life would cost; she bent
down to slake the wound, rigidly staring at the
bullet hole with its pale blue bruised rim to keep
herself conscious of what must be done. They
drove slowly to the street. Mrs. Vosz called out to
Fat to send the doctor out to their place at once.
Ellen Rood got into the car with Mrs. Vosz.
The boy breathed with a short, slack sound. He
seemed to fall lower and lower against the two
women who held him. He kept licking his white
lips. In a voice that was stern, his mother spoke
softly to him.

"Be still; we will get you home; everything will
be all right."

Ellen Rood saw how frank and delicate was
Mrs. Vosz's touch upon the pack bandages that
had to be changed constantly.

The road lay ahead of them in a straight line of
dust. Though their house was one of the nearest
farmhouses to town, they could hardly see it for
the stirred cloud of dust that drifted low on the
land. Mr. Vosz gripped his steering wheel and
asked a question, how Franz was, but his voice
made no sound. Pictures returned to him of the
times of crisis in his family. Always it was his
wife who turned with a heavy strength to meet
emergency and trial. He was weak in adversity.
He thanked God that he had something to do,
such as driving, though the wind carried fine
gritty dust into his eyes, and pitted his cheeks,
and rattled faintly upon the faded surface of the
car.

As they neared the house, Franz opened his eyes
with a look of inquiry. His legs stiffened against
the women's for a moment, a soft tremor that
seemed to press for reassurance. He shook his head
a little, as if to shake free some puzzling thought.

Inspired by Mrs. Vosz's majestic and serene control, Ellen Rood said,

"There!"

to the boy, and at once began to weep. He shut his eyes again and the trembling pressure of his body was quieted. By a secret hysterical suggestion, Mrs. Vosz thought of the track meet where his brothers were running and jumping. Her hands on his shoulders heavied with a terrible resentment that Franz was wounded rather than one of the other boys. She inhaled sharply in rebuke for the thought. The three boys would all gather again at the high school field. They would! They would!

The events were slow in starting, and the contestants strayed over the center of the field, a grassy place which was enclosed by the running track. In the white sunlight, which was filtered by the haze of rising dust, the athletes made a pattern of brilliant color. Their trunks and jerseys were spots of orange, vermilion, yellow and magenta, and white, blue, green and maroon. Their bare arms and legs drew color from all these tints of cloth. The grassy plot was already green, and moving against that and upon the black cindery track, the

boys' shapes and colors leaped to the eye. They
pranced like horses, limbering their legs for the
events. They knelt and practiced starts. Running
backwards, they danced against the wind, serious
and intent upon the science of preparing for races.
The two Vosz triplets paced each other, grunting
under their breaths. They were watching absently
for their brother.

At one o'clock, the starter's pistol sounded,
cracking down the wind, which was rising con-
tinually, making it hard for the runners to breathe
comfortably. The spectators were ranged upon
unpainted bleachers. They were mostly boys and
girls from the competing schools in the district,
though a number of people from town had come
from the Courthouse meeting to watch the con-
tests. They sat facing the mountain, which was
disappearing from its base upward, as the plain
let its surface into the air in a wind of dust. The
sky at the horizon turned a gray white. Above,
it stayed blue and brilliant where the sun stood.

Richard Vosz was announced for the high hurdle event. He trotted to his place in line. At the
sideline stood his brother Joseph, watching him.
Dick scraped the cinder track with his cleated shoes

once or twice, and spat on his finger tips, a gesture of confidence rather than utility. Joe nodded at him. The starter raised his stubby pistol. He glanced at a small crowd of spectators who were just arriving, having parked their cars at the gate. He glanced down at his stop watch, and cried, "on your mark" "set" and fired.

The boys leaped ahead. Excited, the new spectators ran forward to see the hurdle race. They leaned down the track. The hurdlers ran with their heads up, rising with legs spread like wings to take the hurdles. Joe heard his brother's name from one of the newcomers. He glanced, and the speaker turned, and saw him, staring with a peculiar reluctance. Joe looked back at the race again. He saw Dick, yellow head and green jersey above white trunks, take the last hurdle far down the straightaway, and breast the tape in a final lunge. He started to run down the trackside to Dick, when someone took his arm, and looked at him, again strangely, and said,

"Joe, did you know about Franz?"

"No, he's late. Where is he?"

"They took him home."

A sensational communication that ran through

the people spread to the bleachers. They began to
rattle down from the board seats, and cluster
around Joe, watching his face to see what he
would do. They had sympathy, but their curiosity
was more powerful. Joe looked at the faces around
him, where obscure messages were implied. He was
suddenly turned by suspense, like fear.

"What about him?" he demanded.

"He got shot."

Heart DeLancy leaned forward, and came between two people to speak to him. She put her
hands on his arm, and mindful of how much he
looked like his brothers, she was excited so that
her voice quivered.

"He had an accident, Joe," she said, turning to
see the proper understanding of her tact in Rolf
Kunkel's face. Rolf nodded soberly at her, and
Heart continued. "He was sitting in a tree before
the Courthouse, and the Sheriff fired at the air,
above the crowd, nobody knew Franz was up there
in the tree. The bullet hit him, and he stayed
there. He sat there, I mean he hung on until the
crowd was pretty nearly gone. He fell out of the
tree after that, and your mother was there. And
your pa. They took him home."

Joe looked at her in a wild silence.

She said,

"I don't know how bad it is."

Joe felt her fingers on his arm, and saw the faces around him echoing his own expression of fright. Their eyes opened like his, and their mouths dropped. They had seen what they came to see. He flung Heart's hands away and turning, ran down the trackside to meet Dick, who was walking slowly back to the starter's line, pigeon-toed, breathing hard, flushed with his victory and modestly hanging his head with a heavy grace as he walked. He was listening to the poured praises of his schoolmates without acknowledging them. Joe ran up and struck him on the breast, a heavy blow.

"Dick," he said, choking on his dry throat, "we got to go. Franz is hurt bad."

Dick paused a second, then without asking details, he fell in beside his brother, and they ran to the gate, past the crowd, Dick pausing only to grab up his sweat suit. He struggled into the upper half of it as he ran. They started through the gate and down the road that led to town. But Joe stopped, and said,

"We can't run all the way. . . ."

"Here comes Rolf. We'll ask him."

Rolf and Heart were hurrying toward his car. They waved to the boys to wait, and climbed in. The engine started. Rolf backed and turned, and overtook the boys, flinging the rear door open for them to get in. Dick threw himself on the seat, and lifted his legs, pulling on his sweat pants.

Rolf drove to town, where Main Street was thronged. The crowd had broken into small groups. Men stood with men and women with women, among the cars, talking. They seemed to be excited. They shook their heads a good deal, and as each little group separated and went to its various cars, there was an attitude, common to all, that contained grief and anger. Rolf drove slowly through the crowded part of Main Street, and then crossing town headed out to the open country on the other side. Joe sat forward gripping his hands. Dick sat sidewise, listening with him to another telling of the story by Heart. There was bitterness mixed with her sympathy. She leaned over the back of the front seat to talk to the boys. Her excitement of the morning was gone. She remembered her actions with a detached shame, and flushing at her own hysteria among the crowd, she told how the people had driven themselves into a riot, and that Franz had gone up in the tree before any of it started. They had seen him run out on a limb and try to gaze into the Courthouse windows. He laughed and ran back and had climbed higher. They had forgotten him. The sheriff fired into the trees. She remembered seeing some leaves fall, and hearing the strike of the bullets among the thick branches. In some awed fashion, she made an eloquent story of the descent from the tree, and the brothers writhed from concern and excitement.

Rolf sat, large and troubled, driving. His big face with the weak blue eyes was twisted in an agony of sympathy. He swallowed several times, for the lump of sorrow in his neck. The dust, twisting into the car by its speed and the wind, got into his watering eyes. Ahead of them, the sand blew in thickening clouds. They could see nothing, and now found it difficult to hear Heart speaking, in the increased wind. They rode swiftly along in a void of blowing dirt, anxious and impatient. Dick suddenly leaned and hit Rolf on the back, and said,

"Jesus Christ, can't you hurry, Rolf?"

Rolf said nothing, too amazed that he should be abused at a time like this. Heart turned back to the front, knowing she must not look at the fear on the boys' faces. Rolf leaned over his wheel, and the stupid suggestion of him that his body made filled the boys with despair. But he stepped harder on the throttle, and the car, groaning and cracking as it bucked the wind, leaped a little as it took new speed, and the boys sat back, and sat at once forward again, watching for a first glimpse of their house far down the road, which was hazed by the blowing drift.

Now thicker, the sand rose high enough in the sky to obscure the sun, and the light turned yellow, softening everything, and bringing a sharp drop of temperature. Off the plain below the mountain, the wind rose and carried sand, pulling it in a great veil across miles of ground, so that the town could not see the mountain, and the Spring morning disappeared with its freshness under the choking afternoon, that swept its new atmosphere across the whole valley, obscuring everything.

8.

SUNDOWN AND AFTER

CLOSING THE HIDDEN AFTERNOON, DUSK FOUND THE wind dropped, and the horizons clear, and a stillness in the air that was welcome after the choking storm. Ellen Rood reached her home just before sunset. She was left there by the doctor, driving back to town from the Voszes'. As she entered her yard, she called out for the children; and presently they came, meeting her with excitement, confusing her with news of the day's events, none of which she heard, content to know the messages of comfort they gave each other by being together.

The sun was vanishing on the edge of the plain, warming that black shelf of the world. Donald suddenly squeezed his mother's arm and holding his breath from regret, he turned and ran back of the house where the failing light lay even. Twenty feet past the chicken house, he stopped running, and walked on tiptoe, bent like an Indian. He went through the dusty open places he knew among the scrub bushes and grass. His eyes were fastened on the snake. The closer he came, the more strictly he knew that he was too late. He had missed it. The moment toward which he had been working all day was gone. The sun was gone, and the twilight turned softly dim. The snake lay quiet, never to quiver again, as he had seen it quiver at intervals in the hot morning, and shudder under the sweep of the windy afternoon.

But if he had missed watching the snake's sundown death, he need no longer be afraid to touch. He went closer, and turned the snake over with his foot. The wavy coils slid and changed so suddenly, with such a heavy fluid weight, that he jumped back, scared by an echo of life. Then he laughed hoarsely at himself, a catch of breath in his mouth, and toed the snake once more to prove that he was not afraid. There was no quiver. The sun was down. The old snake was really dead. He kicked a few scoops of dirt against the long body, and trotted back to the house, where the light of a lamp in the kitchen made him shiver with awareness of the evening's coolness. The green yellow flare of the gasoline lamp through the window was something that made him feel all of a sudden like a very little boy again, and at the same time, charged him with responsibility, like a man. He quickened his steps, running to the door, needing to be inside, where the yellow lamp shone with quiet clarity upon everything he knew and loved.

Ellen too possessed some feeling of restored security in her kitchen. She laid the Black Maria on the sewing machine and covered it with the newspaper properly. Then leaving her hat and coat, she bent down and pinned Lena's hair up on top of her head, making the little girl resemble a tiny adult. The child squealed with fun. The heaviness in her breast began to melt, Ellen thought. She felt tired and no longer desperate, or lonely. When Don came in, swaggering a trifle, she wanted to laugh out at him for his ridiculous assumption of importance. She sent him for water, and began to gather the sparse ingredients of her family's supper.

Moving at her familiar concerns, her mind became pleasantly empty. The children helped her. They ate their supper without talking, though thought returned to Ellen when she watched the children eat, with hunger and satisfaction in every gesture of their spoons, their mouths, their licking tongues and working cheeks.

After supper, they turned the lamp a little higher, and gathered in front of the kitchen stove where vestiges of fire still bloomed through the velvet ashes. Lena lay in Ellen's arms and Donald sat by her feet, facing her, while she read aloud to them in halting voice that wavered now and then from fatigue. The story was from Grimm's fairy tales, an ancient copy on grey paper with rubbed binding of faded red. The world of swans and forests, deep and treasured obligations in the hearts of princes and swineherds, was a simple and real thing to Donald. His little sister always dozed, breathing like a puppy, with hot nose and petulant little sounds. Ellen read with a monotonous inflection, an expression something like the doleful and vague aimlessness that her singing in the crowd had that morning. But the story always filled her with feeling, and some transfer of that touched Donald.

The evening latened. It was fully dark outside now, and the strange day was ended. Lena lay sleeping behind the fairy book. Don rubbed his eyes to stay awake, and Ellen had briefly forgotten the ride of the afternoon, charging through the dust storm with the heavied body of Franz Vosz held by her and his mother. Ellen knew before Mrs. Vosz that the boy was dead. Waiting for her to discover it, Ellen wondered wildly what to do. The car jolted on, beating against the cross-road wind. Presently they saw the Vosz house through a rift in the dust cloud. Mrs. Vosz petted Franz to encourage him. She found out then.

Small red embers sifted down the grate of the stove. Ellen's voice fell away. Like her children, she seemed ready and willing to succumb to tiredness. Around her, for this moment, were all of the things that let her have peace, however humble they might be. The room was crowded with possessions, none of which had value, yet all of which were valuable to her for the impulse she had to gather them and hold them, some attempt to make with profuseness what she lacked in worth. Her mind wearily and in content turned upon the troubles she faced, along with the rest of the people in the valley. But aside from a feeling that some-one was responsible for her, and must help her, must help everyone in difficulty, she was happy. The kitchen was warm and the children were by her. The lamp faded gradually, as its air pressure in the gasoline bowl lessened. She saw with an intimate pleasure that a pot of beans was soaking on the floor beyond the sewing machine. It was a kind of happiness to feel tired, and to give in to it. She sat with her eyes closed. Her high cheekbones preserved the illusion of a smile on her worn face, though her mouth drooped. She forgot the Voszes.

9.

SOLACE

BY SUNDOWN, FRANZ VOSZ WAS PROPERLY ARRANGED in death. He lay in the front room on an ancient sofa. His face astonished everyone with its difference: he looked hardly like himself, they thought, not perceiving the absence of beauty, the famous splendor which all the triplets had in almost equal measure. Now, with color fallen out of his cheeks, and his eyes shut, his mouth stiff against his teeth, it was possible to see that the boy's features were

anything but distinguished, and that bereft of its
character, his face and body, impersonal, should
fail to echo the things in him that had been loved.
All the late afternoon people came to look at him
in the parlor, and were shocked by this trickery of
death. They would look at the ageless face, and
then consult their memories, and then turn to see
the surviving brothers, to recover some image of
that dead boy that would be recognizable. It was
Franz's memorial, that the eyes of the living should
reject his dead likeness as faulty; and seek for some
less real thing than the facts of his bone and still
flesh, the architecture of his person, and demand as
vestige any reminders of his spirit, made of laughter, loyalty, wit, strength, and easy vitality and rich
temper.

NICE

His father remembered him best.

He remembered exactly the difference in this son
from his other triplets, which was a sly, childish
pleasure in excelling them at everything, and a
modest refusal to do so very often. He remembered
that Franz had been cleverer with people than his
brothers, and that he had also been, so, more inclined to tell lies, and evade bothers, all with the
greatest and most charming blandness. Mr. Vosz

had wept, in silent spasms, when he had driven in to his own porch and been told by his wife that Franz died about three miles back. He had carried the boy in the house, concerned in his mind with stopping his sobs, a first concern of duty and self-consciousness. In the early evening, he received the people who came to call, unable to say anything, but he shook their hands, and suggested with an embarrassed wag of his head that they were to go in the front room and see the body. He was divided between thanks that people should be so kind as to bring sympathy, and resentment that his private grief was so exposed to anyone who might come.

Mrs. Vosz, on the contrary, though she would see nobody, lying inert on her great bed and swelling its shape with her shaking body, required Richard to report to her whenever anyone came, who it was, what they said, if they had messages for her; her mind trivially busy with the social aspect of death in the family, while her heart slowly grappled with the grief that sat there. Her fat hands were fretful, wandering to her lips, or her temples, holding handkerchiefs and pressing her heart. In her eyes, behind the tears that streamed

ceaselessly like a veil to keep her from seeing too
clearly, was a latent spark of comprehension, a
little force that would grow with her memories
until she would know the real size of her loss, a
deprivation that was the greater for her years of
wildly building up its meaning and value.

She heard cars come and go, farm wagons; the
low voices of consolation, the shriek of some un-
canny dog in the yard. She commanded her mind
to invent tasks. Her hands travelled with her
thoughts, and lying in tears upon her bed, she
seemed more active and restless than if she'd been
on her feet at housework. Finding things for
Richard and Joe to do, her voice told them in
hoarse groans. Behind all these devices of evasion
moved images of Franz, of her three sons, whose
epitome he was. She saw him run down the yard
as a tiny child, with yellow hair, and trip, falling,
returning to her with bleeding knees, and a little
face ugly in rage, his tears mingling with the run
of his nose; she remembered his boyish cruelties to
dogs and chickens with a perverse tenderness; how
he looked asleep when his brothers had carried his
cot one summer dawn out to the yard and brought
her to see the joke of his not awakening; she called

back family scenes in which her favour for Franz was clear, like accusation; and at this a new weight fell on her heart, and she half-sat up in bed, calling for Richard and Joseph, who came at once, scared by the terror on her great face that was wet with grief. She put out her hands, and took theirs, staring at the boys with flooded eyes. They held her to a sitting position, and murmured to her, soothing her, knowing that she was wanting to speak to them through the suck of the sobs in her throat. They exchanged looks, adult in their intuition; perhaps this was something worse than sorrow? Mrs. Vosz dropped her head, and said, at last,

"My boys must hate me, but don't ever leave me, he is dead, and I love you both just as much. . . ."

They were astonished. They hushed her, speaking tenderly, and she refused their efforts to quiet her.

"Maybe I have been a bad mother; I loved Franz and petted him, and you boys used to know it. Papa always said he was my favorite; oh Dick," she cried, "maybe I have been unfair? Joe? You won't leave me?"

The boys blushed with wretchedness. They read
in her eyes the fear that she might be abandoned
by everyone now. It was less remorse and love for
them than it was a feeble and pitiful fright lest the
two sons she had slighted now feel free of her. Her
body, working in the bed with restlessness, her
reddened face, touched them with some humble
return to the time of their dependence upon her,
and they promised with a moved enthusiasm never
to leave her. They convinced her, and she fell back
again to weep and deny the pictures her mind
made for her.

She finally let them go to see who had just
arrived, and who was leaving. Outside her door,
the boys looked at each other with an emotional
shyness. A feeling like shame took them both.
They went in and looked at Franz, seeing with
memory the neat bullet hole in his chest, dark,
rimmed with blue that faded to the white flesh.
The visitors made the proper clucking sentiments
around them. Their father hung his head and
shuffled his feet by the door. Andrew Lark, in the
corner, rocked faintly in the walnut runner-rocker,
and declared to anybody who neared him that
Franz Vosz had been a fine lad and a proper; and the

brothers stood knowing without thought or word
what missing Franz would be like, all things from
their birth having come to them equally and with
the same meaning for all three, having grown up
closer than together. They shivered within their
best clothes. By staring long enough, they could
imagine Franz breathed.

Andrew Lark stirred and rose, slowly, when his
wife told him they'd better be going. She was
mindful of the proprieties, and they'd been there
too long already. The old man paused again to look
at Franz, and knew a recognition like joy flood his
mind; he saw a self-image at the same age, and
passing Mr. Vosz, Lark was heartier than ever, in
his ancient way, at the conviction that Franz was a
fine and proper boy, going out with his wife and
feeling a curious exhilaration.

But as he was leaving, a car drove into the yard,
and the Sheriff came to the porch, and Lark
turned back to see.

The brothers held the door against the Sheriff,
instantly speechless. Their minds cleared, and they
saw how soft and silly they had been. Their grief
found its true nobility in a masculine, animal rage.
It was the man who had killed their brother. They

began to growl and whisper promises of what re-
venge they would invent and commit. The Sheriff
put his hands against the screen door, and said
softly, "Now listen, boys; listen"; and the limited
commotion brought their father to the door.

Vosz thrust the boys away and opened the door.
He grasped the Sheriff by the arm in a painful grip.
Without speaking, he brought the Sheriff into the
front room, through the dwindling crowd of visitors. They stood by the old couch and they both
looked down. Vosz was a reasonable man; he hated
the man beside him, and he knew any blame was
foolish. He watched the Sheriff, who looked at
Franz. Perversely, Vosz was angered when the signs
of genuine grief showed in the Sheriff's face, and he
felt this to be some intrusion upon the privilege of
those whose loss it was.

The boys had gone to their mother's room,
raging with the news. Mrs. Vosz opened her mouth,
a shape of outrage. Now Mr. Vosz came in and said
the Sheriff wanted to see her, and here he was.
There was a shuffle of feet at the bedroom door,
as Vosz stood aside; and the Sheriff came in to
stand at the foot of the immense bed and feel his
tongue cleave to his dry mouth as he gazed at the

mother of the boy he'd killed. The brothers stood
at the head of the bed. Richard was in the near
light of the lamp, and his body cut off much of the
light on the figures in the room. But Mrs. Vosz,
struggling against her pillows to sit erect, was
bathed all down her left side by a gold flow of light,
that spilled on cheek and loose bosom, and the
white of the bedclothes. Dark shadows lost her
other side and put shapes on the wall. The silence
in the house was full. Mrs. Vosz stared, shaking
her head with the slightest movement at the Sheriff.
The tears ran silently down her face and into the
hunched hollows of her neck. She seemed to be
sexless and without age, in the beautiful strange
light, and in the attitudes of astonished grief she
held, an almost impersonal embodiment of emotion, and without being able to say it or imagine it
in words, the Sheriff thought that for the first time
in his life, he was looking at the face of suffering,
and he felt a new sadness for the messes into which
people got through no fault of their own. He
looked at the brothers, who were pale in the lamplight with hunger for vengeance. Vosz stood beside
him, saying nothing. The Sheriff said, hesitatingly,

"There's hardly nothing I can say, Mrs. Vosz.

I *have* to say I'm sorry, and you know and I know and his father knows it was an accident. But we all know *that* don't help matters none. But I *want* to say that I'd trade places right now with that boy if it'd do the good of giving him back to you. I *swear* I mean it, ma'am?"

His voice was rusted with confusion, and his words coming slowly had the dignity of entire sincerity. He let his fingers rest on the foot of the bed. Mrs. Vosz closed her eyes and allowed her head to fall back so that her thick neck swelled out at the sides. The loose hair drifted down to her cheeks. She made no sound. The brothers leaned to her and put their arms against her back, to support her. The Sheriff was made mean in feeling, to be so ignored, and he spoke again, with pleading rough tones.

"I maybe was out of place to come here, ma'am? but so long as I didn't come to pay my respects, I figured it was worse than coming where I'd be mighty unwelcome."

She opened her eyes and stared at him again. Her lips drew in against her teeth, as if to make her silence more terrible, more accusatory than ever. No one in the room took his eyes off her.

There was a groaning splendour of grief about her shapeless body and her blotched and quivering face. In the front room, the visitors were as still as the dead, their eyes glistening toward one another as they listened for the furies that must be loose in the bedroom.

"Anyway," said the Sheriff, moving back from the carved walnut of the bedstead, "I can't tell you how *I* feel, but I know how *you* feel, Mrs. Vosz? and I swear to God A'mighty that . . ."

He could not say what he would swear.

He was sorry? The word was too little. Guilt? But his crime was not a crime. Mrs. Vosz leaned forward a trifle, as if waiting, extracting, the full dues of his misery. Her eyes went sharp, behind the run of tears, and she fatly stirred in her bed to await the avowals that were so hard for the man to make. The Sheriff turned to Vosz and shrugged. He ran his thumb up and down the lapel of his coat. He turned back to Mrs. Vosz, and saw with a fresh eye the ugliness of her abandoned body, and his feelings rose up in him with resentment that she should so refuse his poor offer of sorrow; he shook his head at her, and dropped his look, while the tears blurted into his eyes and a sob lost his

breath. Mrs. Vosz leaned sharply, to see these sig-
nals of feeling. He turned and left the room in the
same appalling silence she had met him with. He
was followed by Vosz, who saw him to the front
door. The visitors had retired to the shadowy corners of the front room and they saw the depar-
ture through the hall doorway. The front door
slammed, and the dogs on the porch whimpered.
They heard the motor start, and saw the headlights
switch on through the windows. The backing and
turning car threw an arc of light across the windows, printing shadows of lace curtains upon the
peering faces. The whine and settle of the changing
gears receded. It was silent again.

But only briefly, for rising in a sob of lost control, they heard the voice of Mrs. Vosz break forth
in a storm of volubility.

She was sitting up, clutching at the strong arms
of Richard and Joe, pouring out an almost word-
less fury of sound. They could recognize in her
thickened speech references to the man who had
just left; they could perceive snatches of pictures
in it, as if memories suddenly showed amongst the
rages in her mind, and demanded expression. They
squeezed her arms and stroked her hair, calling her

to be quiet. The tears ran from her eyes and the saliva poured from her lips. She sweated and strove with her hands to say what was in her heart.

The sounds of this fury came to the front room as something terrifying, and a few of the women tiptoed to the bedroom door, full of an awed courage that demanded a sight of such grief. What they saw made them feel either sick or hysterical. The two boys grew frightened and exchanged impassive looks that included the notion of flight; but they would have denied it, and they heard the voice of their mother change, taking on the noble and witless sonority of one who prayed at a camp meeting. She made the shapes of visions in the air with her hands, and her voice became solid over the caught gasps of the sobs, and her husband came into the room to see upon her stained and wretched face some light like the light of those who receive the Holy Spirit, and he knew that she had found occupation in the old assurances of her Baptism. Her voice rolled on, like the river of a sermon. He fell to his knees by the side of her bed and put his head on the bedclothes and began to weep. Her hand descended upon his skull, and he felt its vibrant obsession.

Richard and Joe suffered for the way their parents had let go. They started to withdraw. But the mother embraced them with her rich tide of wrath and redemption, making them kneel too, rising in some majesty of strength above the shames and the griefs of her men. The voice poured on, filling the air with threats and judgments, phrases of hatred and promises of peace, the blood of the Lamb and the fires of Hell, with amen and amen and alleluia.

In the front room, Andrew Lark once again brought his wife to the door. The evening was clear, and as they drove away, the harangue of sorrow and comfort was still going on.

10.

SURVIVAL

FROM FAR DOWN THE ROAD, ANDREW WATCHED FOR
his mill, and when he saw it, sharply edged against
the last sheets of light that faded down from the
deepening sky, he felt an uprise again of the exhilaration that had possessed him back there as he had
gazed upon the dead boy. Mrs. Lark rode beside
him, her hands folded in her lap, her eyes working
right and left, right and left, as she told over in
sympathy the terrible meanings of the house they

had come from. She could tell herself that everyone had their time; it was best to meet it without
terror; but when a grief so monumental as Mrs.
Vosz's got loose, it went extra deep into hearts that
before had known few doubts.

They rode, the old couple, bouncing in unison
as the old Ford bounced. It was an ancient car,
with a spidery look to its thin axles, its steering
gear, the supports for its windrattled top. If anything could make it look more precarious and
tentative than it really was, it would be to see
Andrew Lark, himself so ancient, driving the Ford
at its fastest speed, an old engine of potential destruction, driven by an old man whose steps must
surely be numbered.

Beside him, Nona was murmuring the slow
words of one concerned with proper misery. He
hardly heard her. He sat driving, his eyes fixed
upon some point farther than the road, his sharp
old mouth that bent in the middle with a look like
a lion's snout grinning with content. When he
turned into their own yard and brought the Ford
to a creaking halt within its shed, he heard Nona
sigh heavily and watched her walk across the yard
with her rheumatic, rolling gait. By himself, he
stood in the cool yard. The wind had dropped.

Above him the mill hardly turned, and he was thoughtless of it. In the late dusk, he stood like some old tree. When he saw the lights from the lamps catch and increase from Nona's match, he cleared his throat, and brought himself out of the curious haze of joy that had possessed him at the Voszes', and went to the back door where the cats were clustered hungrily, mewing and climbing against one another, and purring when Andrew opened the door and let them through the shuffle of his feet.

He dropped his stiff black felt hat on the kitchen table, and went to the front room. There was his newspaper, all set right by Nona on the table. The lamp made a live world of a circle of light, cutting across the red plush of the sofa, dropping to the green and brown carpet, crossing the black boards of the floor, the seat of the gold cane chair, and the dusty black of the coal scuttle. He heard Nona talking to the cats. He sat back in the morris chair which had adopted his shape like a shell, the green corduroy cushions hollowed for the curve of his long back and the settle of his bony rump. He heard Nona begin setting supper ready. He admitted he was hungry.

He went when she called him, and sat with her

at the kitchen table, and as the evening advanced
with his silence continued, she began to worry
about him. He was looking at nothing, only smiling, as if for himself, eating his eggs and scraping
his porridge spoon and wetting his chin in silence.
To make up for this strange look of his, she began
to chatter, lamenting that such things could happen as happened today; she spoke of the time her
son Elbert had died, as a child of three, and she
said she could feel for Mrs. Vosz; to lose a child
not yet grown, hardly, was so sad; she heard Andrew chuckle, and raised her eyes to him. He
seemed to be alive with pleasure, some happiness
which dismayed her.

"Andrew:" she said, putting her freckled old
hand to his arm, "what's got *in* you!"

He shook his head, and shoved his chair back,
and returned to the parlor and his big chair. In
the orange glass miniature of a top hat he found
toothpicks, and took one, and began raking his
bloodless gums with it. She came and peered
through the door at him, ankled by her cats, and
was alarmed to see him lying back with his eyes
shut, smiling and working his toothpick. She saw
the paper at his elbow, ignored; and the change

from his habit of hastening to read after supper
filled her breast with a breathless fright. She went
in and picked up the paper, and laid it on his lap,
speaking to him. He scrambled for the paper with
his fingers, and didn't open his eyes, only nodding.
She left him, troubled by strangeness. In the
kitchen a new fear took her, and she remembered
that he had left his glasses on the windmill platform that morning; that Moses was supposed to
have come out that evening to bring them down,
and that the events of the day had prevented their
seeing Moses. She thought, If Lark goes up there
at night . . . He'll fall . . . and she folded her
hands for the fool she had been in reminding him
of his paper, for he would need his glasses for that,
and in his musing and smiling, he could sit forever without them.

She silently went to the back door, and walked
to the foot of the windmill. Her face was hot with
a wild courage, but she looked up at the clear
towering lines of the timbers, and said to herself,
with feelings like weeping, "I could never climb
it." She put her hand on the low rung of the ladder,
as if to test her strength. The mill softly keened
above her, and she looked up at it, seeing its blades

against the chilling sky where the stars were bright-
ening against the darkness. She shivered; it would
be another cold night, and embracing her shoulders, she went back to the kitchen. Andrew was
motionless. She went to her work of clearing up,
listening for the moment when he would sit up
and clear his throat, and declare that he must get
his glasses down from the platform.

But her fears were stretched over the whole
evening.

He sat, content and silent, in his big chair.
When she came to sit with him and do her sewing,
he looked at her. His eyes were remote and milky
with odd meanings, and she decided not to ask
him what he was up to. He could not have told
her. He only knew that an inner sensation of
power and life possessed him. It had arrived in
him in the late afternoon, when he had looked
down at the dead Franz Vosz, and seen so young
a man, with so appealing a face, with such a strong
body, laid useless forever; while he, Andrew Lark,
who would never see seventy again, was alive and
could feel the blood flooding his veins; and the
things he knew filling his mind; and the things
he saw coming into his eyes. He had shaken his

head over the dead. And then he had admitted
to himself that he was proud to be alive. He had
thought of himself at Franz's age, looking at the
boy. The whole chain of things that had happened
to him in his life began to come back to him. His
memory was prodigious. He saw how fortunate
everything had been. If there had been any devia-
tion from the line of his history, how different
everything might have been!

But it wasn't.

He was conscious of his old age. The only triumph of old age, which is survival, lived in him
too. He sat and mused all evening, shaken and
enlivened by the happy selfishness of his own
thoughts. The boy was dead, and Andrew felt an
unmalicious satisfaction in finding himself still
living. He forgot his paper. Every time he looked
at Nona, when she recurred in his chain of memories, he wondered why she looked so perplexed.
He would chuckle at her, and she, still possessed
by thoughts of grief and worry, would be shocked
at his levity, not knowing how he was welling with
contentment, a sense of integral being.

He thought once of mentioning what was in his
mind to Nona. But he sensibly decided that she

would never understand him, and he closed his
mouth again, after frightening her by holding it
open for speech for a long moment. He only
shook his head at her fussy inquiries, and sank back
into preoccupation with his content.

The cats came suddenly to life in the kitchen,
and raced out from under the stove when the clock
struck ten. The day was over, and Nona was relieved at last, for he would never climb the ladder
now, it was too late to read. It was bedtime.

She went to the kitchen and let the cats out for
the night. They paused on the doorstep while she
held the screen door open. They tasted the night,
turning their heads whose little faces were hooded
by ears and neck. Then, with silent accord, they
turned and became parts of the shadow along the
house.

Andrew rose from his chair, obedient to his
nightly ritual, reflecting that it was just such regu-
larity of habit that had brought him this far and
that would take him years and years farther. He
guessed he hadn't missed a minute in years from
getting ready for bed at ten o'clock. Nona, in the
bedroom, moved against the area of the lamplight
like a sleepy and comfortable shadow. He appreci-

ated dimly the wide and the heavy bed where so much of his joy and content had come to pass.

The yard was cleaned by the wind of the day. In the chill moonlight, he looked around, as he had looked around every night for so long. He spread his legs and began to piss, yawning sleepily. He made a little river on the swept ground. He shivered, feeling the cold strike into him, and anticipating the warmth of bed. Inside, Nona, hearing his nightly watering of the ground, shrugged with impatience, her delicacy offended, reminded by this of all the little things that a lifetime with Lark had never reconciled her to. But they vanished from her mind out of habit when he returned to the house, chuckling and peering at her sidewise, saying that he'd forgot to get his glasses down off the windmill. Nor had he missed them till now. Now what did she think of that!

He trundled by her, pulling at his shirt with little grunts. She thought with an almost shamefully girlish notion how foolish he was, how much doing-for he required, and, remembering the Voszes, how if his need of her should be broken by death, she would know nothing to do but wait.

He let himself into bed, which creaked. He held

up on one elbow, listening intently. An idle night
breeze was about, and he thought it might be
enough to make the mill swing around and screech.
But he nodded his head with satisfaction when all
he could hear was a constant, airy w'anging from
the metal blades that turned slowly, and the metal
fin that strove always to be parallel with the wind.

11.

FALLEN IMAGE

THE EVENING RUSH WAS OVER BY THE TIME ROLF and Heart pulled up at Fat's Cafe. The light from the restaurant streamed across a limited area of sidewalk, with a golden spill that suggested warmth after the sharp and coldening evening. They went into the Cafe and Fat waved at them with his bare arm, a figure of buoyant good feeling, addressing them as Folks, and piping in his oily voice. He came around from behind the counter himself in-

stead of letting Mrs. Rocker take their order. They
sat down at a table opposite the shining coffee urns,
and looked up at Fat hungrily.

"I've had such a rush," said Fat, "don't know
hardly what's left; but you can bet, you can just
bet on it, I'm gonna feed you."

He cocked his eyes at them, looked at them
shrewdly, a regard that made Heart drop her eyes
and inwardly admit the embarrassment and the
confusion in her breast. Rolf told Fat to bring
them whatever he had that was *good*, and turned
back to Heart.

She looked straight into his eyes, and pulled a
blush from his veins. They were both breathless;
when they started to speak to one another, their
words had a catching pulse under them. She laid
her hand against her breast, thinking that was
where her desire lay; but it eluded her touch, and
she stirred in her chair with the possession of her
feelings. Rolf hung his head. They had been driving in the car ever since they left the Voszes'.
Without saying much of anything, the two of them
had arrived at their conclusion, and Rolf knew it
was Heart's strength that she had excited him, and
with caresses and no words, had proposed to

him the things that would happen after their
supper.

It was warm in Fat's Cafe. The steam rose and
whispered above the hooded stove. Presently Mrs.
Rocker came with the thick white bowls contain-
ing the soup, flanked by crackers, that always
heralded Fat's "Club menus." She walked with
exaggerated care, her miserable slippers creaking
and yawning at her every step. She bit her un-
toothed lips with a grin of pride and caution, and
at last set the steaming soup down before them,
and retired behind the counter to consult Fat with
one of her willing looks that so enraged him.

But tonight he sang in his heart. He seemed
beyond rage, for that was the sign of a weak man
who was not master of his world, and therefore of
his temper. Fat was hard tonight. He narrowed his
small eyes, and squinted into his stew with pitiless
and rocklike character. He turned to instruct Mrs.
Rocker to set some celery on the table for the
guests, and lifted his eyebrows at her in an elabo-
rate threat which she failed to recognize as such.
Hard? Tonight. He would fire Mrs. Rocker tonight. The crowd from the track meet had filled
his cash register. "Mrs. Rocker," he thought,

"here's your wages and a little over. Good-bye, git.
Git out, Mrs. Rocker, I said. Go on, git now, I said.
You old fool, can't have a smelly old woman like
you round here no more, I said. Waagh! whoosh! I
said, and don't try no cryin and weepin and cater-
waulin, I said, on me, I said, it won't do you no
good 'tall. I said, I put up long enough with your
cussed foolery, and wastin time, and taking my
wages week in and week out, I said. Go on, I said,
git! ——"

He sliced some bread, warmed and enriched by
this mental achievement of a scene he was waiting
for with relish. He sent her to the table with the
bread, and then leaned on his immaculate counter
to watch the diners. His fat arms and pink elbows
flattened out on the light yellow wood. Feeling
hard, serene, a master of all situations that might
touch him, he prided himself tonight on a keen,
even a relentless understanding of other people.
They might have secrets from some, but not from
him. His own secret was so well guarded that no
one would ever know it: who had seen him? In all
that crowd? Nobody. He had picked up a brick,
a loosened brick from the edge of the walk in the
Courthouse plaza, and in a moment of glorious

inspiration, he had risen above the crowd and
hurled the brick at the doors, smashing the window, creating a leadership in destruction that
through no fault of his own had been put down.
But he, Fat, was the single hero of the day's events,
though nobody knew it but himself; which was
enough. His private virtue flowed throughout his
immense and dainty body, a masculine elixir.

Heart and Rolf ate their supper in half-silence,
consulting one another with small sounds and
quick glances. Their breath lay under their words
like soft laughter, and Heart could hardly eat anything. Rolf consumed everything as it came before
him. She watched him eat, feeling possessive of
him already, and noticing with a strange intensity
such things about him as might at other times have
disgusted her, his clumsy table manners, chewing
with his lips open, packing his food with his knife,
ways that were unCalifornian. But to her, a pre-
ciousness seemed to cover everything about him;
and in his mind, as he inarticulately preserved the
heat that had them both, was some tenderness that
covered his resentment at having been so obviously
trapped and excited by her.

Fat played his fingers along his mouth, leaning

on his palm and watching them through drooped
eyes. There was solicitude in his heart, as he made
idle and pimpish dreams about the two young
people. He felt like offering them congratulations,
with sly winks and tribal pokes in the rib for Rolf,
and a shared reference to their common valour as
masculine achievers. But he only hummed his little
tune, and stored up the interesting moments, im-
agining voluptuously what Rolf and Heart would
do when they went away alone after supper;
leaving him alone with Mrs. Rocker, who would
then be canned with grandeur.

He looked around from the diners when he
heard the front door open slowly. He left his chin
resting in his palms, his elbows planted in rings of
their own fat upon the counter. His eyes narrowed,
with the keen feeling he had had since noon. The
door closed slowly and respectfully after a thin
shaking man who walked down the aisle between
the tables and the counter. His large head was
unsteady upon its small neck. He was smiling, his
lip lifted off his teeth by a scar. In his hand he held
a scrap of a hat. Fat watched him approach, saying
nothing, only turning his head to keep his eyes on
him. Heart looked up, but didn't recognize Leo,
and forgot him.

"Excuse me, mister," said Leo, in a breathy whisper, shaded with an attempt at charm and culture, party manners, "is there anything you could spare me to eat? I'm broke, and pretty hungry, I can tell *you*."

Fat drummed his fingers against his teeth. A flush like a smile rose around his eyes. He said, with a lazy mildness,

"*Nuh*-uh,"

meaning no by it.

Leo stood. His constant sensation of quivering showed a little in the way he moved his arms in a motion of appeal, as from one man to another.

"I won't need very much," he said, looking around at Heart and Rolf, and then at Mrs. Rocker, with a smiling abandonment of pride and independence, a public resignation of his only birthright. "I'm hitch-hiking my way to California, where I have relatives; my uncle is a lawyer there, and once I get there I . . ."

"*Nuh*-uh," repeated Fat, yawning artificially behind his hands. Mrs. Rocker stared at Leo with compassion. Her hands worked under her apron.

"Once I get there," continued Leo, "I could probably send you some money for what I might maybe owe you. Boy, I'm *hungry*."

A hearty idiom like that, coming in Leo's faded voice, brought tears to Mrs. Rocker's eyes. She was astounded when Fat stood up suddenly, leaning across the counter, and bawled in his thin forced voice,

"Nothing here for panhandlers and handouts! Now git!"

Fat subsided back of the counter, and turned his back, inventing business with sweeping the crumbs off his meat block where he also cut bread.

Leo turned around. The scar was frankly part of a snarl now, and his smile showed dry as the lips stuck to his teeth. He shuffled down the aisle toward the door. There he paused, having a ridiculous trouble in getting the knob to turn and the latch to open. Heart and Rolf lifted their heads, and Mrs. Rocker encouraged the temper in her heart. Fat scraped the crumbs over and over into separate little mounds. At last the door opened and Leo went out. The door slammed after him. Mrs. Rocker saw him turn up his collar against the cold night and move off into the shadows. She looked at Fat. He refused to look at her. He was saying to himself, over and over, "That'll show them," not knowing whom he meant or what was to be shown, except that he was tired of being imposed on all his life by people, confusing his weakness which came from within with impositions which came from without.

Three minutes went silently by. Then Mrs. Rocker rolled off her apron and dashed to the door and into the street. She stared up the walk after Leo's direction. Fat turned and screamed to her, "You come back in here!" hating her for acting upon the impulse that he had denied. She moved out of sight. Everything changed for Fat. The image toppled. He said to Heart and Rolf,

"I'd have done it, only if I feed one, I feed all. God knows I hate to see anyone go hungry. . . ."

Heart shrugged, a sophisticated gesture that was unconscious; she was thinking of nothing but herself.

In a moment Mrs. Rocker came back. She was remembering Leo's smile, a vehicle for hatred. She said she couldn't find him. He'd disappeared. He sure had looked hungry. She looked at Fat, shyly, with a trusting simple smile. He scowled at her and then sighed. He went flabby and weak again. Everybody else did what he wanted to do, and should have done. There she stood, not even

thinking badly of him because he had turned
away a starving hitch-hiker! Her watery blue eyes
never concealed any opinions. If she had been
momentarily furious, needful of feeding Leo, it
was all gone now. She watched Fat for her in-
structions, and took every little idle movement or
expression of his as a signal of some kind for her.

She went to get the dishes from the table, and
prepare for dessert, which Fat set out on the
counter: two pieces of pie, cherry pie, of his own
make, with thick juice running slowly from the
crust to the plates. He laid squares of cheese on
each plate. But Heart suddenly stood up, and Rolf
stood with her. They said they didn't want any
dessert. She smiled. Able to conceal nothing, yet
secure in their sphere of excitement, they left the
Cafe. Fat put his pieces of pie back into the icebox.
Mrs. Rocker performed her nightly tasks before
closing-up. At last, when he stood waiting for her
to get into her hat and coat, his pockets full of the
money emptied from the cash register, he looked
at her and dropped his look, knowing he would
never fire her; she trusted him; she relied on him;
she thought he was o.k., even after Leo; she made
him sick of the sight of her. He held the door

open, and she walked out. He locked it, testing
the latch a time or two. He felt abandoned, knowing it was his cherished self that he had abandoned.
Mrs. Rocker walked her way, opposite to his. He
turned and ambled up Main Street. The few stores
were dark. The money clinked and rustled in his
pants pockets. He was lonely and lowered in his
own eyes. There was only one way in which to
regain himself, to lose himself. Thinking pitifully
of the waitresses in El Paso, with their blue eyelids, their black lashes, the fiery rouge that bloomed
on their cheekbones, and faded to the neck in a
powdery plaster white, their yellow hair, their
amiable hips, he left Main Street and trudged
through the dust and leaves of the back streets,
walking under the great hooding cottonwoods that
strained the cold starlight, and came to the faded
green board house that sat low behind a rotting
fence. The windows were heavily curtained. There
was no sign of life. But he walked to the door and
rapped. In a moment, with a final question of folly
in his mind, he was admitted.

12.

CONVICTIONS

THE DARKNESS WAS PUNGENT WITH THE SMELL OF printer's ink and rolls of newsprint, mixed with years of dirt swept into the corners of the newspaper offices. In the middle of the rear wall was a door that had a window in it. The glass was filmed with a pearly dust. Through this the faint moonlight filtered. There was no other light. Heart moved to the door and tested the key in the lock again, to be sure the door was fastened. She heard

Rolf stir and breathe where she left him, sitting on the long bench that was covered with her coat. She felt again the loving clumsiness of their hands, meeting and offering expressions of what was inside their hearts. Standing in the moonlight away from him, she saw her fierceness go, and marvelled that his should survive, should even grow so that his embraces seemed to her shameful in looking back on them, though she had desired them and brought them to being.

He called her in a whisper to come back beside him.

She walked slowly over to the bench and sat down. They could see each other like shadows, in the dimly distributed moonlight. He was not replete yet, not content, though from the moment of their slipping into the dark printing room, using his key at the back door, her abandon had asked physical questions. Not seeing her in the dark, she seemed to him a stranger, losing the sharp diffidence, the resentment in her eyes. He had not expected such wild tendernesses as she gave him. But now they had been given, she was again changed; and sat beside him on the bench in propriety, some seriousness that perplexed him

and inclined him to anger. After all: he thought:
there can't be any airs or secrets any more now.

"What is it:" he said to her, setting his large
fingers on her breast.

She shook him away.

"Oh, I don't know," she said, in a wretched
whisper.

"Aren't you glad?"

"You hurried me. . . . I couldn't think."

He sat away from her, wondering if she really
thought that. The sound of a soft sob convinced
him that she did. Compassion and pride bloomed
in his breast. He leaned to her again, and this time
his touch was delicate and mournful.

"I couldn't help myself," he murmured, relax-
ing finally from his lust, taken by the new emotion
of being a slave to his passions. She sighed again,
and in a throe of tenderness and weakness, put her
head on his breast. She resigned herself. She felt
that she had a right to be weary, for the months she
had been in bringing Rolf to this night. He stroked
her hair, richly confused by feelings of lust and
protectiveness, warmed by one and inspired by the
other. But nothing he could say, his murmurs
about the joy it would be to have other nights, the

fact that they were not lonely any more, could make her stop her faint distress.

"What is it:"

"What have I got to look forward to now:" she said.

"What do you mean?"

"You know, well enough. . . ."

"No, really I don't."

She pulled away from him.

"Well, I know . . . I know just what I mean to you now, after this."

He remembered that there had been no words of love exchanged.

"Oh, come on," he said. "You know you'll mean more than ever to me now."

"Oh, I know that," she said. "But in what way: any girl will know the same thing."

"Well, if you mean will I go looking around after other girls, you're just crazy."

". . . not what I mean."

"Then what:"

"You won't have any use for me but in one way, now," she said, feeling sincere in the ancient ritual.

"Oh:" he said, his voice hushed as he realized

his obligation. He hotly thought that she had led him on, God knows she did that. All afternoon, talking and hinting, and working on him, with her hands, and then being silent, she certainly had led him on. Her voice cut against his secret accusations.

"What could I do, Rolf darling? You knew I couldn't fight against you, you knew that. The trouble is, I love you, if I hadn't loved you, it would have been easy to turn you down. You know that."

Here it was. In terror, he stated that he loved her. He said that was why he had done what he had done. She embraced him gently, and waited for the other avowals to follow. She shuddered against his breast, making whispered references to his powers, the fact that he was overmastering, and even dangerous. In the intimate darkness, surrounded by the familiar atmosphere of his job, printer's ink and the acrid tone of linotype metal, cooled, everything she said seemed likewise familiar and believable. Perhaps, no, certainly he was overmastering. It seemed to him intelligent and logical when he declared, later, that they would be married right away. He told her he wouldn't

hear of any objections, there was too much non-
sense nowadays about women and freedom.

Heart closed her eyes, clutching his large shoulders. She had known her advantage and used it.
He was convinced, even if she was not. She knew
how he would act the husband, and that she would
spend her life preserving for them both the illusion
that he was a delicate tower of strength, whose
control was capricious and dangerous. He would
believe this himself, and it was only human to
drink in a heartening belief about yourself, she
thought; she also thought, closing her lips upon
him to deny it, that her various inner convictions
of truth and plan would accompany her, disappointed, though happiness could live over that.
Holding each other, delivered to one another, they
sought terms in which to declare their shared lives.

13.

CONVIVIALITY

HAZEL BROUGHT FAT OUT OF HER ROOM INTO THE sitting room at the back of the house. She walked in front of him, sighing with a comfortable propriety, and closing her thin kimono about her loose body. He followed her, sorry for passion vanished so soon, and stepped through the portières in the doorway. Hazel threw herself on a chair and crossed her legs, waving Fat to a chair at the table where there were a bottle of whiskey and several glasses. Two men who were sitting at the table looked up at Fat in a moment of silence. He recognized one of them as Do Miller, and said hello.

"Hi, Fat," said Do.

Do turned back to his friend. Both Do and the other man were sitting at their ease, in their undershirts, with their pants loosened, their shoes off, and their shirts and coats hanging on the backs of their chairs. The stranger had a cigar which got in the way of his words. But he spoke in a continuous stream of interest in himself, and what he had done, and was going to do.

Fat poured a drink and listened. Hazel yawned, and lighted a cigarette, smiling at Fat through the tears of smoke and fatigue. He felt suddenly very fond of her, and saw her with new eyes, as if she were not a whore, but someone whom he'd met in somebody's home. Remembering his half hour with her, he blushed. He turned his nose into his whiskey glass to hide his feelings. The liquor was sharp, a cheap grade of white mule. It made him gasp for a second. But with Hazel and whiskey, he was full of comfort. He belched loudly, a surprising thing for Fat to do, and Hazel, knowing him in his Cafe, knowing his elegance, the daintiness of his ways, laughed aloud at him, and stood up, pushing her hair over her forehead with both hands.

"Great big boy," she said, in a teasing voice. She turned and ran her arms down across his shoulders from behind. But a rap at the door interrupted her, and she squeezed his breasts and left. Fat settled down to listen. The stranger turned from Do Miller, whom he had been tapping on the chest to punctuate his stories, and looked at Fat with a friendly smile, as if to include him in the audience. Fat smirked. He heard the front door open and close, and then the sound of walking down the hallway, and another door.

"I tell yoh 'baout dis mawnin?" said the stranger. Do shook his head and drank from his glass.

"Baout dat nigga?"

"*Uh*-uh."

"Boy howdi!"

The stranger dropped his head and laughed weakly, flopping his hand at Do as if to defy him to think up anything better than what was coming.

"What nigger?" said Do.

"Dis mawnin: I was pumpin tah up, lost all the

air outa my spah tah, and nis nigga came along.
I reckoned he was one onnem hitch-hikin niggas,
and I figgad givem a rad to town. So I tolm get
aholt onnat pump, pump up my tah for me."

Fat leaned out on the table, flattered by the way
the man's eyes sought his every now and then,
dividing his story between Fat and Do, seeking in
vanity for the applause of both.

"Well, ol nigga stan nere, and tell me he won't
pump no tah. I looked at im, I said get aholt. Nigga
begin to grin and laugh, and said he didn want
pump no tah. Boy! Bam! did I hit im! zowie! I
hit im so fast on each side of his jaw, he didn know
what's coming or goin. I backed im up against the
car, and I hit im again, swingin low, and he begin
to cry. He cr-y-y-y, just like a puppydog. I told im,
nigga, I says, put up yoh hands. You hit me, I says.
Come ohn, hit me, nigga! Should of seen 'at nigga
try. . . . Hit me, I says. An' I let im have it
again."

The man took his head in his hand, closing his
eyes and wagging, voiceless with amused memory,
and full of sociability. Do Miller grunted in his
chair, a sound of appreciation, and slumped lower
to be comfortable. The stranger looked at Fat with

dancing eyes, and Fat winked at him, and slapped the table top with a crash of his fat paw, drawn into the world of men who destroyed insolent negroes, and enjoying the membership.

The talker threw himself back against his chair again, and stretched out his legs, scratching his groin, a gesture of self-congratulation.

"So, nigga, he try to hit me. An nen I get sore, well, not sore, but it made me mad, to have at nigga try to hit me. So I backs im up towards de ditch, and boy! howdi! did I let im have it! I knocked him down wid one blow, and nen made im stand up again." He smiled with modesty, his red handsome face looking strangely younger. "After he stands up, I knocks im down inna ditch, an boy! he's inna ditch for good! Knocked im out pretty as you please! He was a young nigga, musta been baout tweny-tweny-one. He had a good build on im too. Be a good nigga, if someone just teach him his lesson or two. Like I did."

He chuckled affectionately. Do splashed some more white mule in their three glasses, and they drank together, full of a common excellence, a power that made them enjoy one another, and that gave them a common point of view. Fat was flooded by sensations of ease and ability. Clearing his throat, a test of his thin tubular voice, he leaned forward and with exaggerated caution, began to tell a dirty joke. Do and his friend leaned forward to catch it. Fat knew they liked him. Their eyes and mouths echoed his own expressions as he told the story. They hung on his lips. When he finished, telling the end through laughter that he tried to control, they all threw back their heads and barked and coughed with amusement. They had found their common tongue. They sat drinking and smoking, solemnly rotating their turns to tell jokes. Each one was finished with the same raking laughter. Fat kept thinking, It does a man good to let go now and then.

Presently the portières were held up and a new girl came in. Her face was chalk white, with rouge spots on the cheekbones and blue shadows on the eyes, and a bowed mouth whose painted outline left the natural one. She had a bony nose, that looked as if it had once been broken, and that gave her face the look of a parrot, when she rolled her eyes and shook her yellow hair. Fat had never seen her before, but had heard there was a new girl at Hazel's.

She walked to the back of the stranger's chair, and leaned down over his shoulder. Fat watched her with a quiver of envy and admiration. She reminded him of the waitresses in El Paso. Her voice sounded now, a smothered sound as if her broken nose interfered with her speech.

"What're you doing?" she said, rolling her eyes at each of them in turn.

"Telling stories," said Do. "Do you know any good ones?"

"I know plenny bad ones," she said, and squawked. "But I never tell them to gennamen."

She uttered this with tones of refinement. The stranger smiled up at her, and she patted his cheek. It was like a little passage between married people.

"Where's Hazel?" she said, with a restless sound in her voice.

"Somebody came in, she went back there with him," said Fat.

"I can't see it," said the new girl.

"See what?" said Do.

"Hazel: can you? How any man could *look* at her, she so *ordinary* looking, I said to myself when I *come* here, My God, do you have to work under

the same roof with *that!* She's so ordinary looking!"

Fat was startled. But, unable to make an opinion for himself, he began to view Hazel in his
mind from this new angle. All he could remem-
ber was her general friendliness, a thing that always appealed to him. But he would never feel
the same about Hazel again, having heard a doubt
expressed about her. The new girl seemed some-
how superior now, and he leaned forward to get
her eye, and began to tell her the first story he
had told the men. She listened to him, shifting
her gaze from his eye to eye, breathing with her
mouth open, waiting with short breaths and widened nose for the point of the story, an image of
appreciation and encouragement. Fat blushed
with content. His voice rose. When they all lost
themselves in new laughter, he lay back in his
chair drunk and reassured.

14.

TO

CALIFORNIA

THE MOON RODE HIGH, UNHARRIED BY THE WIND and the cold that played along the ground. The road banked with the hills, far, far in the distance, and rose invisibly toward the mountain passes. The mountain itself was a shadow against the lighter shadow of the night sky, and Leo looked ahead now and then, trying to set his gaze steadily upon the dense and inscrutable darkness where the mountain opened and the road entered, a place where his steps must eventually carry him, though he murmured to himself in a little high moan that he felt so tired and hungry. . . .

It was the shocking coldness of the night that made him begin to wonder at his decision to take to the road, trusting for some kind of hitch to carry him nearer California. The afternoon had been whipped by wind and blown sand. But the morning, with its heat, had told of Spring. To-night there was an edge like Winter in the air. He leaned into the direction he was taking, and breathed against his turned-up coat collar, making a warm mist of spittle. His hands were folded inside his shirt on his breast, and the fingers moved constantly, crawling over one another on his bony arch. His lips moved to the tune of the thoughts that rolled in his mind. (He had the conviction that he was striding firmly toward the mountains; that he would walk into the dawn somewhere beyond the dark canyons of black pine; that his promised land of California awaited him with warmth and money, kindness, a job, security. It was the place where his uncle lived, and all the movie women, where life was a thing of easy solutions and sunshine on the seashore and beauty that was cheap and available. He saw his arms swinging and his head thrown up. The road was a river of moonlight.)

Moving by the ditch-side, Leo's feet hardly travelled. He was shuddering within his loose black coat. The strain of his eyes to watch for the beam of a car's lights, a car that might pick him up and let him sleep to the rumbling rhythm of tires on a graded road, the feeble cracking of his fingers against his chest, the way he was turned and worried by the fall of the cold air on the mild wind, all these made him look like a scarecrow blown fitfully, an image of public humour and no significance.

No cars came and went. The high moon softened all objects with a silver pour. Leo's eyes watched the fence posts, his feet trembling after one another as he walked. It had taken him hours to get so little beyond town as he was now. He imagined that he could see strange things in the richly shadowed ditch above which he was walking. Thoughts of fear intruded among his sensations of speed and accomplishment. But he would bite his tongue and widen his eyes, remembering that he was from a good family, with a good background. He was an educated man. He had ideals. He was practical enough to go out after them, he told himself. Hence California.

Suddenly he found himself sitting on the edge of the ditch, retching emptily against his palms. He was tossed on his back by the strain of convulsion, and then he sat up again, feeling strangely more comfortable, and with a cleared sight. He looked around him and winced at the cold that fingered his skin through his clothes. He thought of lying down in the ditch to be out of the wind; and he crawled down into it, but it was capriciously filled with tumbleweeds by the wind of the afternoon, and he recoiled from the sharp burrs and thorns of the billowed, brittle bank. He pulled himself erect by a fence post. There was a dark shape in the field beyond the fence. He leaned on the post and focussed his eyes. What he saw was the body of an old Ford, a burned-out wreck that sat on the ground without wheels or top, no fenders or doors, only the rusty and dull black shape of the body, and the shapes, inside, of the front seat and the back seat. On the ground were scattered bits of débris from the wreck, old fenders, a lamp reflector, a shattered door, a

broken wheel. In the pouring moonlight, these
things shone clear.

"A car," said Leo to himself aloud. He raised
himself to look better. He said that it would at
least break the wind. He could lie down in the
back seat and be out of the cold wind. There would
be some protection under the curving back of the
car's body, and there was no danger that he might
be run over in that field, as there would be if he
lay by the road to rest.

Feeling joyful, he decided to climb through the
fence and go to the wreck. He lifted himself a
little, raising his leg to climb over the barbed wire.
He fell to the ground, astonished by his weakness.
He could not pull himself up to climb the wires.
He began to whimper, fearing that he would never
reach the wrecked Ford, where he would spend
the night. It had become the image of haven to
him. He was too tired to change his plans. Bitterly
setting his hands against the ground, he began
to roll and crawl nearer the fence, and with a
faint warmth of success, rolled under the lowest
line of barbed wire and saw himself free in the
field. He came to his hands and knees, and then
arose, slowly, standing airily. He picked his way

among the flung junk of the wreck, and reached the body. He rejoiced to discover that the rear seat cushion was there, left by the owner because it had been half burned up. There was still an old smell of fire about the wreck, and where Leo touched the metal and the charred upholstery, his hands came away black. Rust had followed fire. The wreck had sat in the field for weeks.

He clambered up into the tonneau. He lay down on the rear seat, and pulled his knees up to his belly. He heard the wind sing like a low gong as it stroked the charred fenders that lay beside the car. The wind passed over his head, and he gratefully lowered his chin to his shoulder, feeling the flow of comfort like a little child, while his hands kept on shaking and his touch on his own face was too chill and remote to be felt.

He had the idea that lying here, he was able to rest for the night, and still be headed right in the morning, for California. He was comforted by the fact that he was below the level of the wind. Nor could anyone see him, from the road. There was nothing to disturb him. He was half aware, later, of a car going by on the road, whistling against the cold with its speed, and touching roadside objects with vanishing light as it passed. (It made him think briefly that his own car, where he was lying, was moving swiftly down the road to the mountain. But he laughed at himself and repeated that he was not riding, he was walking.)

While his body, curled against itself and stiffening with cold and sleep, lay dark in the tonneau of the burned-out Ford, his dreams picked up from his thoughts and went on. He was walking toward a sky that was like sunrise and sunset. It was warmth to wrap himself in. (His face quivered and his eyes wept a little stream of liquid that glistened in the vast moonlight.) He dreamed that the sea was breaking at his feet on a shore of warm sand, and beautiful women crossed his dream, familiar in the black and white of the movies; American goddesses never before within his grasp. The dream's unreality was his only strength, but it was sufficient, against the night that grew colder as midnight passed and the still late hours followed. Sometime before dawn, Leo's dream ended. He died among its images, which came out of his deepest wants.

He lay in his car, in some way a responsibility on all the lives he had ever known; though when

the farmer and his hand found him days afterward, it was with simple expressions of wonder
and curiosity, deciding that he had died of ex-
posure on the night the frost had cracked down
on the valley.

maybe, the failure is in the author.)